# CORRUPTION

THE NEW PRESS | *International Fiction Series*

# Corruption

———

TAHAR BEN JELLOUN

Translated from the French by Carol Volk

THE NEW PRESS · NEW YORK

*L'Homme Rompu* © ÉDITIONS DU SEUIL, JANVIER 1994
ENGLISH TRANSLATION BY CAROL VOLK © 1995 BY THE NEW PRESS

LIBRARY OF CONGRESS CATALOGING-IN-PUBLICATION DATA

Ben Jelloun, Tahar, 1944–
[L' Homme rompu. French]
Corruption / Tahar Ben Jelloun; translated by Carol Volk.
p.          cm.
ISBN 1-56584-295-2
I. Volk, Carol. II. Title.
PQ3989.2.J4H6514   1995
843´dc20                                    95-11667
                                            CIP

*L'Homme Rompu* ORIGINALLY PUBLISHED IN FRANCE BY ÉDITIONS DE SEUIL
PUBLISHED IN THE UNITED STATES BY THE NEW PRESS, NEW YORK
DISTRIBUTED BY W. W. NORTON & COMPANY, INC., NEW YORK

Established in 1990
as a major alternative to the large, commercial publishing houses,
The New Press is the first full-scale nonprofit American book publisher
outside of the university presses.

The Press is operated editorially in the public interest, rather than for private gain;
it is committed to publishing in innovative ways works of educational,
cultural, and community value that, despite their intellectual merits,
might not normally be commercially viable.

The New Press's editorial offices are located at the
City University of New York.

book design by HALL SMYTH

production management by KIM WAYMER

printed in the UNITED STATES OF AMERICA

96 97 98  9 8 7 6 5 4 3 2 1

*J*OWE THIS BOOK TO PRAMOEDYA ANANTA TOER, A great Indonesian writer now living under surveillance in Jakarta and prohibited from publishing.

Upon arriving in Indonesia, I tried to meet with him to show my solidarity and express my admiration. I was advised not to see him; my visit could cause him trouble.

While there, I read his novel, *Corruption* (translated into French by Denys Lombard and published by Éditions Philippe Picquier), which appeared in Indonesia in 1954. As a tribute to him and as an expression of support from one writer to another, I wrote this novel (originally entitled *L'Homme Rompu*), a novel about corruption, an affliction now as common to countries in the South as well as the North.

The story takes place in contemporary Morocco. Under different skies, thousands of miles away, the human soul, worn down by the same misery, sometimes gives in to the same demons.

T. B. J.

𝒯HE BUS IS LATE, AS USUAL, AND WHEN IT ARRIVES, IT'S filled to bursting. Mourad looks at his watch. He can decide to shove his way onto the bus, crushing some toes in the process, or wait for the next bus and risk arriving late at the office. Mourad, however, is always on time, more out of principle than neurosis. Two options remain: he can take a taxi to work—which will cost ten dirhams, the price of two packs of Casasport Blues—or walk and arrive panting. He's been wanting to quit smoking for a while now, more to save money than out of pity for his lungs. At his last checkup, the doctor at work told him, "For a smoker, your lungs are clean." That was all he wanted to hear. But when he walks a long time or climbs stairs, he's out of breath, and that the doctor doesn't see. So he decides to take a taxi, vowing never to buy cigarettes again.

The driver is in a bad mood. He keeps lowering his window and spitting into the street, shouting insults. Mourad doesn't dare ask what has gotten him so mad. He is talking to himself, then turns to Mourad and says, "I've had this taxi for ten years, and can you believe I'm still paying off the man who got me the license? What a bastard! I work day and night to pay my debts. I don't see him anymore, that bastard. He got his money, but now I owe my uncle, who loaned it to me. It was either that or nothing."

Along the way, Mourad does his daily calculations: "Taxi, ten dirhams; lunch, thirty-three dirhams; five for coffee; five for cigarettes; fifty-four for Wassit's geography book; and then at least a hundred dirhams to take the little one to the doctor, and that's not counting medicine. Basically, I can't get ahead. As usual. I know it, and even if I forget, there's my wife. Hlima will remind me."

AT THE OFFICE, THE *CHAOUCH* — THE ERRAND BOY — BARELY says hello. Here the warmth of the greeting depends not on your rank but on how much extra the job brings in. Mourad is an engineer. His role in the administration is to study construction plans. Without his approval, no construction permit. It's an important and much envied position and it comes with a pretentious title: Deputy Director of Planning, Prospects and Progress — after all, his engineer status, for which he took part of his training at a French school, and his bachelor's degree in economics from the University of Mohammed V in Rabat must be acknowledged. On his modest salary he supports his family, pays the rent and his children's school expenses, and also provides for his mother. But he can't make ends meet. He lives on credit, thanks to his grocer, and knows he can't have a third child. They can say all they want that every birth is an asset, that God will provide for the needs of his creatures. Mourad is adamant on this subject, and to put an end to the discussion insisted Hlima start using an IUD. It was then that she told him, angrily, "Your assistant is a real man! He earns less than you but he lives in a beautiful house with two cars. His children go to the French mission school, and he also takes his wife on vacations to Rome! All you give me is an IUD and meat for dinner only twice a week. This is no life. Our vacations at your mother's, in that old house in the medina in Fez — you call that a vacation? When are you going to realize how miserable our lives are?"

"MY LIFE IS WORSE THAN MISERABLE," HE THINKS TO himself. Is it my fault that everything is going up, that the rich keep getting richer while the poor like me are stagnating in poverty? Is it my fault that the dry season has made the poor even poorer? What should I do? Steal? Swindle people out of their property by convincing them that real estate is a bad investment?"

As he thinks this, his assistant, Haj Hamid, enters whistling. "Good morning, boss! Did you have a good night?"

"I'm okay, thanks."

What he hates more than anything about this man is his arrogance and his smile, with its sly air of complicity. Even though they're not in the same office—a door with windows separates them—he's exasperated by this person. He doesn't like his sweet cologne. He has to open the window to get rid of the smell. He also doesn't like the noise his chain bracelet makes when he writes. Haj Hamid is the antithesis of a culti-vated man: he's probably never read a book, though he spends a good hour every morning reading the news. Mourad wonders how one can spend so much time reading such empty newspapers. Maybe he doesn't read them, maybe he's only pre-tending, putting on an act. From time to time, he comments out loud, things like, "Saddam, now there's a man!" Mourad feels like responding, saying, for example, "Someone who sends his people to be massacred for eight years in Iran, then does everything in his power to provoke a war with half the planet, that's your idea of a man?" But no, he prefers to keep quiet, and in any case he has no choice. If he starts a discussion with Haj Hamid, he'll have to go all the way, leave out nothing. There are things he notices but chooses not to mention, like, for example, the visit of Mr. Hakim, a rich landowner who likes to speak in metaphors and insinuations. He often spouts proverbs, some of which are beautiful and enigmatic, such as, "The minaret has fallen, the hairdresser has been hanged," or, "Kiss the hand you cannot bite." Mourad knows that deals are being made outside the office. Mr. Hakim comes here just for show, to bring documents and take others away; the stratagem doesn't escape Mourad's morose yet watchful eye. Then there are the gifts—sacks of wheat, cases of fruit, lamb for Aïd el Kebir, the festival of sacrifice. All this is attributed to the generosity of peasants. Haj Hamid is very appreciative of these gestures, made just like that, for nothing. No denunciations, no accusations, no secret reports. In any case, there's no proof. Corruption is, by its nature, not immediately visible. Unless one sets a trap, but Mourad isn't shrewd enough for that. He doesn't have the soul of a cop, no matter how strong his desire is to cleanse the country of these practices. True, he's the boss, yet he notices that his power is being threatened. True, he signs papers, but who's to say that other deals aren't made verbally, secretly. One would have to live day and night with Haj Hamid, not let him out of one's sight. No, that's impossible. Fortunately they're not in the same office. He is boring, self-satisfied, and vain.

Mourad remembers the story of the Egyptian policeman who had decided to move in with the person he was keeping under surveillance. Their cohabitation ended badly. The person under surveillance wound up killing the police officer. Mourad doesn't want to die for this slimy assistant, perhaps the only one in the entire office within the Ministry of Development to use brilliantine in his hair. That too is unbearable. That smell of rancid oil. Maybe one day Mourad will strangle him. In any case, he won't get a promotion. Of course, he doesn't need one, his salary is merely symbolic. A few thousand dirhams a month don't pay for trips to Europe and his little biannual pilgrimage—umra—to Mecca.

The chaouchs like Haj Hamid. He's generous, talkative, attentive. He keeps up with their problems, helps them out, gives them his old clothes, thinks of their children at the holiday season. He's a good man. On Fridays, he leaves the office at eleven to go to the mosque. On this day, he arrives all dressed in white: djellaba, shirt, trousers, slippers. After prayer, he goes to lunch and returns to the office a good half-hour late. Mourad says nothing, but he jots down these latenesses and dates them. You never know. Perhaps one day Haj Hamid will be summoned before the Disciplinary Committee, which may lead to court. But that almost never happens. Nonetheless, he remembers a cousin who had spent a large part of his life teaching, until the day he became an inspector and discovered the possibility of earning extra money by cashing in on his inspection reports. He had barely begun getting rich when he was denounced and arrested. He tried to justify his behavior to the examining magistrate by saying that people's low salaries were inciting them to corruption. He prepared a fairly detailed report on what he called the parallel economy that fills in the gaps left by the state, and ended up calling for the legalization of "personal contributions" as a means of advancing the country. His fancy discourse just served to sink him even further. He was condemned to five years in prison. Three years later he was set free, full of rage, and promptly disappeared. Some say he is trafficking in narcotics, others claim he's emigrated to Canada, where he sells fake Persian rugs.

There is also that mysterious visitor, a tall, bald man who calls himself Marrakchi. As soon as Marrakchi enters his office, Haj Hamid gets up and goes into the corridor with him. He apparently finds these visits unpleasant; afterwards, he is often in a foul mood. Mourad believes the man must be blackmailing Haj Hamid. He would like to unravel the mystery, question this man and eventually use him as a witness. But that's impossible. Mourad is a peaceful man. All he wants is to ensure his children's future while maintaining his dignity. He is ready to make any sacrifice, but not to violate his principles and do like the others. Nonetheless, he does have brief moments of regret, remembering the wad of banknotes that a real estate developer, Mr. Foulane, once placed on the table of a café for him. There must have been ten thousand dirhams there. With that kind of money, he'd buy a moped, a dress for Hlima, and holiday outfits for each of his children, take them all out to a restaurant for a fish dinner, smoke American cigarettes and maybe even buy himself a Montecristo No. 1 cigar for eighty dirhams, the price of two meals under normal circumstances. All he would have had to do was sign, just one little signature at the bottom of the page. But no, he wasn't for sale. He'd gotten up and left the café, furious. Mr. Foulane had caught up with him. "But I was told that ten thousand was enough... If you want more, we can arrange that, take this as an advance and you'll get the rest after you sign..." Mourad had looked at him and spit on the ground. "I don't take bribes."

Had he been furious because someone had doubted his integrity or rather because deep down he regretted having so many scruples? This question still plagues him. He absolutely must not speak to his wife about the bribe; she would probably throw him out the window. Her bursts of anger are frightening. She sews at home to make ends meet and often curses her luck. Her sisters all married wealthy men and live well, while she married Mourad, whom she met at the university, for love. As soon as they married, Hlima got pregnant and was unable to continue her studies or take a full-time job. Things slowly got worse, especially under pressure from her family.

She could live in peace with a husband of modest means, but her entourage looks out for her interests and pushes her to protest. Her father says nothing. He appreciates Mourad and knows how serious and honest he is. Her mother is a hypocrite. She smiles at him, but makes fun of him behind his back. She finds him small-minded, poor, and dull, and never misses an occasion to make a snide remark: "Sidi Larbi is getting a new car, I could ask my daughter to talk to him about selling his old one to you at a good price. How much could it cost? Fifty, sixty thousand — that's nothing by today's standards!"

Sidi Larbi is just the type of person Mourad despises. He's a wormy lawyer who's gotten rich off car accident victims; he makes a deal with the insurance company, gives a share to the victim's family, and divides the rest among a small circle of agents. He flaunts his wealth and sleeps very well. He's capable of falling asleep anywhere and at any hour. He eats fast, burps, and naps, snoring. Money comes in from every direction and nothing bothers him. As far as he's concerned, Mourad is a failure, a poor guy, unable to adapt to modern life.

IT'S TRUE, I'VE NEVER BEEN ABLE TO ADAPT, AS THEY SAY. What is adapting? It's doing like everyone else, closing one's eyes when necessary, putting aside one's principles and ideals, not preventing the machine from turning. In short, it's learning how to steal and share the benefits with others. Personally, I can't do it. I don't even know how to lie. I'm not shrewd. I know that what they call "the machine" doesn't work with people like me. I'm the grain of sand that gets inside and makes it squeak. I admit to liking this role. It's rare and precious. I devote myself to it even though my wife and children don't live all that comfortably. It's my pride and joy, but I know it won't do them much good.

Anyway, what can I say? All I know is that my mother-in-law is not only a hypocrite but that, with all due respect, she would have made a good madam in a brothel, and in fact she married her daughters off not according to their suitors' moral or intellectual qualities but according to their financial prospects. You might say she sold her daughters to the highest bidders. Of course it all happened in a roundabout way, veiled, indirect, never straight on. I'm the only one she abuses, since I spoil the picture. I'm her mistake, the one who shouldn't have gotten into the family. She'd told her daughter this but ended up giving in, counting on my eventual adaptation to the machine. I've disappointed her. I remain passive, calm, without getting agitated. My wife's screaming, however, is hurtful. She doesn't understand me. There is no solidarity between us, no complicity. We're poor and have no business living beyond our means, as if we were rich. It's simple, but she refuses to accept the truth. She bugs me, constantly comparing us with others. I hate when people compare things that aren't comparable. There is a gulf between Sidi Larbi and myself. We have nothing in common.

Why did I marry Hlima? I often wonder. I search my memory to reconstruct the fateful moment when this decision was made. I'm not even sure I was the one who made it. My hand must have been forced. I notice that often a man fairly rapidly and even lightly makes a decision of great importance and seriousness, without realizing that he is pledging away his most precious possession, his freedom, and in certain cases his entire life. This same man would think for hours before making the most ordinary purchase, hesitate between two shirts or two ties, ask the advice of a friend or a mechanic before choosing a car.

I have the impression that I didn't even have the right to hesitate or think about it. The fact is, Hlima was the oldest of her sisters and therefore had to be married off as soon as possible to liberate the younger ones. We met at the university; I liked her luscious lips and large breasts, which I fantasized about like a child. I wanted her. I wanted to satisfy my sexual urges. She was there but refused to give herself to me. The price to pay was clear: marriage, for in her family you didn't touch a man outside of matrimony. She leaned forward as she told me this, her marvelous breasts partly visible for a few seconds, then she stood up and told me, winking, that she liked my nose. This surprised me. It was the first time anyone had said anything to me about my nose, which is just ordinary. I found it amusing. I relaxed and took her hand, which I brought to my lips as I had seen Cary Grant do with Ingrid Bergman. It was my fifteen minutes of romance. I thought that life was a movie. I could see it, my movie, on the big screen, in black-and-white, with jazz music, Duke Ellington on the piano, and me drawing near, my heart pounding; Hlima in cinematic close-up, her lips trembling, closing her eyes to receive her first kiss, falling into my arms, while from the corner of my eye I watch the clock, because she has to be home before her father.

Our movie lasted several weeks. We didn't have any place to go. We took refuge in dark cinemas for our flirtation until the day her brother caught us. Then and there I understood that in order to have some peace, the relationship had to be made official. Once and only once were we alone and almost naked, in the room of a friend who had left me his keys before going away for the weekend. She wore me down. I had to fight to get her to take off her clothes. I succeeded in pulling off her bra, but she kept her panties on. Already she was stronger than I was. She wasn't going to give her body to me; I had to conquer it, and the only means was the legal route, the one that would chain me down for life.

When her brother came to see me at the entrance to the university, I knew it had all been arranged between them. The cinematic interlude, even the room my friend had lent me, it was all a set-up. Her brother was supposed to have surprised us, but, by chance, or luck, he had gotten the floors mixed up. But all this doesn't explain to me why I married her. True, I wanted her, but I knew little about her family.

Was it love? My shyness, my hang-ups, and my seriousness were handicaps to knowing the truth. Now, I know that I desired her physically. At the beginning of our marriage we spent a lot of time making love. What was surprising was that she went wild in bed. She made love with her entire body. One day, from underneath the bed, she pulled out the book of Sheikh Nafzaoui, a manual of Muslim erotology, and decided that for one month we were going to execute every position described by the sheikh, twenty-nine in all. It was funny: we made love with a manual in front of us. She knew this book by heart and recited entire passages to me. I memorized a few names of positions I found comical, like "black-smith's copulation," "the camel's hump," "Archimedes' vice," and so on. Why the black-smith? At a certain moment, while the woman is on her back, "her knees raised toward her chest so that her vulva is exposed, the man executes the movements of copulation, then removes his member and slides it between the woman's thighs, like the black-smith removing the red-hot iron from the fire…"

We had as much fun reading as we did trying to put Sheikh Nafzaoui's advice into practice.

Twenty-nine ways. One a day. But on the whole they're all fairly similar: the man always on top of the woman.

When her period came, she lay on her stomach, put a cushion beneath her to raise her buttocks, and I gathered she wanted me to penetrate her that way, a position that was not in the book. I think the sheikh discourages approaching the woman at all during menses.

I refused to perform. I don't like sodomy. That was the day I was treated to my first attack. "You're not a man!" she told me, getting up. I was sitting on the edge of the bed, my penis shriveled. I felt ridiculous and understood that with this insult, and my failure to react to it, my life, before long, would be transformed into a hell.

The next day, I tried to have a discussion with her about the previous evening's incident. It was a waste of time. She had her own definition of virility and I was stupefied to learn that physical violence, blows, were one of its signs. She asked me to hit her while we were making love — a far cry from the gentle, romantic kiss between Cary Grant and Ingrid Bergman. We had fallen into the everyday grind. She informed me that she was pregnant and that during this time, I was requested not to touch her. I confess that this prohibition suited me fine. I slept alone, in the living room, and began thinking of Najia, my cousin who had just lost her husband.

With Najia it was love. I loved her voice, the gentleness of her gestures, the pleasure she took in talking about the books she was reading, the sense of decency that came out of our times together. I would see her almost on the sly, when she came to visit my mother, her aunt, in Fez. She would accompany her mother there, and while the two sisters talked, we would sit together on the terrace like kids and chat. At the time she was engaged to a young doctor. She loved him. I knew this and didn't dare mention my feelings. When she would ask me about Hlima, I would give vague replies. I didn't want to get her mixed up in my problems. I could have been more aggressive, and maybe I would have married her, but my mother said she was my "half sister"; she had supposedly nursed her while Najia's mother was sick. I don't know if that's true. In any case, it was the main reason given; maybe the two sisters didn't want a marriage between cousins and used this subterfuge to discourage any attempt at a liaison.

Najia rarely sees her father, who married a second wife.

Now, when I think of Najia again, I measure the breadth of the mistake I made by marrying Hlima, who would have been happier with a brute or a corruptible man.

I remember the first years, when I began working at my office within the Ministry of Development. Hlima was the first to suggest that I demand a "commission" for each permit I signed. It was one of our most violent arguments. At the beginning, I tried to explain to her that corruption was a cancer that was eating away at the country and that my upbringing, my sense of morality, and my conscience were firmly opposed to the practice. Again she told me that I wasn't a man! This time I laughed; she couldn't bear it and began throwing things at me. To quell her hysteria and calm her down, I thought of her as a fire; I ran to the bathroom, filled a bucket with water, and emptied it on her. This was extreme. She sat on the floor, her entire body wet, and began to cry softly. She mumbled things like, "I'm telling you this for your own good, for that of your future son: if you prefer to stay poor, that's your business, but I can't stand poor people..."

We weren't poor at the time; we lived modestly. Occasionally I thought of changing jobs. With my engineering degree, I could have gotten hired by a private firm. For that, one needed connections, to know powerful people, to be from their world, from their class. So I didn't try. It wasn't for lack of ambition, but more out of shyness. That said, I have never been shy in the face of people who try to bribe me, and am proud of it. There's never been a crack in my resistance. Finding myself face to face with a man who is trying to buy me gives me strength and courage. I don't preach. I stand up and kick him out of my office without saying a word. The man backs out the doorway while I, without losing my cool, return to my desk and continue my work. This is how I earned the reputation for being "a man of iron." But for the others, I was the "grain of sand."

One day I amused myself by jotting down the various ways in which people had tried to corrupt me. There was the one who had placed on my desk the title to a parcel of land on the edge of town. Then there was the one, a simpler fellow, who delivered two superb lambs to my house on the eve of Aïd. There were also the two cases of Johnnie Walker — to this day I still don't know who sent them. Once I received an invitation to dinner at a well-known restaurant, an offer I was weak enough to accept. A woman showed up in place of my host; she was beautiful, and professional. I also received an airplane ticket for a pilgrimage to Mecca, *umra*. I returned it to the sender without a note. There were a certain number of gifts for my wife and my children: jewelry, clothing, games, a dog, a cat, a horse, and even a parakeet. These were all amateurs. The shrewder ones went through Haj Hamid. While I was working conscientiously, signing only those applications that met the criteria, Haj Hamid was negotiating behind my back. When I rejected a file, he was always the one who brought it back to me with all the necessary documents in the days that followed, requesting my signature. I was doing my job without suspecting anything, neither that my assistant was abusing my trust nor that he had his own little sphere of influence.

I was neither a man of iron nor a grain of sand, but simply an honest man.

But for the little people, I was neither iron nor sand. For them I was a saint. That's what a young doctor who had just been named to the city's large public hospital told me one day. He was even more naïve than I was. I'd met him the day I brought Wassit to the emergency room after he'd swallowed something toxic. I noticed that the attendant responsible for signing people in was neglecting my son's case and making us wait without telling us why. He was a stout man and rather pretentious. He had the nerve to diagnose patients and direct them where he wanted. I noticed that he shook some people's hands more than once. They were "greasing his palm," as they say. In the meantime, people like me, who didn't understand the system, were waiting in the draft of a dirty corridor. So I raised my voice. He didn't care. I demanded to see the head doctor; he laughed. He turned his back on me and gave the impression of being very busy. A doctor who was passing by, the one who was to become my friend and who saved Wassit, stopped and asked the nurse for an explanation; he gave none, shrugged his shoulders, raised his arms to the sky and said it was God's will.

I later learned that this attendant was a powerful man. He had grown rich by "taxing" patients; he also sold them medications and sometimes sent them to private clinics, which paid him a commission.

I filed a complaint with the head doctor for nonassistance to a person in danger. I received a response thanking me for my testimony. I realized that this attendant had a great deal of influence and couldn't be touched.

It was at this time that one of the top health officials, himself a doctor, was discovered diverting supplies purchased by the state for the hospital to his private clinic. It was also at this time that the same man was found to be preventing certain medications from crossing the border because the Swiss-German manufacturer refused to pay him a commission. This man, later removed from his position, now lives peacefully off the revenue from his clinic and his private income, despite the fact that he was responsible for the death of hundreds of patients.

I dreamed of retribution from the sky. I made plans in the course of my sleepless nights to stop this individual and have him judged by an honest, independent tribunal. I dreamed of a court martial, of justice for the people. I dreamed of a national cleansing; a magic hand would pass over the people, bringing order to this society in which ultimately anything goes. I turned my dreams over in my mind until I was stricken with laughter or a fever.

THE DIRECTOR CALLS ME IN. I FINISH A REPORT, STRAIGHTEN my files, adjust my old tie, and tell Haj Hamid that I'll be in the boss's office. I should mention to you that the boss is rarely in. He has so much to do, he grants us little of his time. He's a decent, self-taught man who is curious about everything. He likes talking literature with me. He knows I have a library and that I prefer reading to television. He also knows my temperament. But he gives me what he calls "a lesson in flexibility" every time. "You have to be rigorous and strict, especially in our country, but a little flexibility doesn't hurt," he often says. "It depends how far one bends!" I answer. We laugh and turn to other matters.

One day he sat me across from him, ordered tea for himself and coffee for me, and asked me to listen to him closely without interrupting: "This is between men, between friends. I have respect and esteem for you. You work hard and your salary is low. You deserve twice, even three times what the state pays you. You really are poorly paid. Your salary depends on a fixed pay scale, and, as you know, the state can't give raises to its workers."

He stared at me during the long, ensuing silence. Then, as if he had recorded a speech, I heard or thought I heard the following. In fact, his eyes were speaking to me in silence:

"The cost of living is going up. There's nothing we can do about it. You have to adapt. Everyone knows that most salaries are symbolic. The state knows it, just as it knows that people have ways of compensating for what they lack. It closes its eyes. It has to; otherwise there would be a revolution. Citizens participate in whatever ways are available to them to fill the gaps. It's normal. It's a national consensus, a balancing mechanism. The whole trick is to do it discreetly, even elegantly if possible. That's what I mean by flexibility. The state should be grateful to all citizens who come to its rescue. It's people like you who ensure the stability and even the prosperity of the country. I grant you that certain economic departments suffer from this practice; I'm thinking of Customs and the Tax office...

"What you are placing in the realm of morality and what you call corruption I choose to call a parallel economy—it isn't even underground, it's a necessity. I'm not saying it's good, I'm just saying we have to live with it and stop confusing compensation with theft. And don't think that only developing countries experience this problem. Look at the scandals in France, Italy, even Japan. Here it happens on a human, individual scale. In those countries, it's no longer compensation for the people, it's the misappropriation of large sums, embezzlement, organized crime. And have you noticed that since Italy has been fighting large-scale corruption, its economy has broken down? There's no comparison between our entirely small-scale and underdeveloped way of freeing up a file to save time and create jobs, and the numbered Swiss bank accounts European politicians open to stash payoffs for the compromises they make with industrial and even Mafia figures. Next to this, we are miserable, underpaid bureaucrats engaged in a daily struggle so that our children can have a normal education, decent vacations, a life without deprivation and sadness. We're not even gluttons. We just want to eat our fill. It's legitimate, entirely legitimate, Mr. Morality! I hope you've understood me!"

The silence lasted a good five minutes. I told myself: a boss doesn't talk like this. It's impossible. It's not his job. It's still me or my naïve conscience talking. It's a big talker. Too many silences to interpret. Too many insinuations to translate. I made no comment. I thanked him, murmuring, "We don't have the same vision of things."

THIS TIME, HE'S NOT IN A GOOD MOOD AND BARELY SAYS hello. Usually he presses me for news of the children. A file is sitting on his desk. Upside down I read: *Sabbane.* He asks me what happened with Mr. Sabbane. I laugh. In Arabic the *sabbane* is the person who washes dirty laundry. The name suits this man. I think a moment and say:

"I think this gentleman was among those who wanted to buy me off. Naturally I had to refuse and he thought he wasn't offering me enough. I found that intolerable."

"And where's your flexibility?"

"I have to learn, sir," I tell him.

Upon returning to my office, I remember that I have to fill out an application for my eldest, Wassit, to be accepted as a boarder at the high school to prepare for his exams. At home there's no room for him to do his homework and study. Like millions of young Moroccans, he studies on the boulevards, beneath the bright lights of the lampposts. I know that if I fill out the application and send it by mail, he won't get the grant. His file won't even be opened. He needs "connections," as they say. I don't know anyone at the ministry. You have to look for connections; it seems it's not necessary to know the individual personally. All you have to know is whom to address and how to slip him the notorious envelope.

Never! If I start corrupting others, there'll be no reason for me to obstinately refuse envelopes. If my wife heard me thinking out loud, she'd say, "You think you're a saint, a hero. Well, you're the only one, and you drag us into your solitude, with its deprivation and need, to boot. Your lords and masters are real men, they think of their children's future and find ways to provide for them. Meanwhile you store up your scruples as if you could eat them! In any case, our son will not be the victim of your inflexibility. I'll do everything I can to make sure he gets the grant."

What is "everything?" Sell her jewelry? Borrow from Sidi Larbi? Flirt with the bureaucrat at the ministry? The thought of it makes me blush. Hlima is incapable of such a thing. No, the devil makes me think such thoughts—I have to put them out of my mind. Yes, she's still young and beautiful. Maybe she cheats on me. It's strange, I never thought of that before. Maybe she's ranting and raving because she'd like to, but her upbringing prevents her. In any case, the day she stops pestering me I'll have to worry: she'll have found someone to satisfy her needs. I've noticed from those around me that men don't have regular mistresses; they like changing bodies and not getting attached. I think of Najia, my forbidden cousin. She's lived alone since losing her husband in a car accident between Rabat and Casa. He crashed into a truck that was stopped on the highway, at night, with its lights out. Sidi Larbi handled the matter; I discreetly intervened so he wouldn't embezzle half the indemnity. For once, to show me he could be honest, he didn't steal.

Najia is beautiful. She's the one I should have married. We could have consulted a *sharia* specialist who might have authorized the marriage despite the drop of shared milk. She's one or two years younger than I am. Maybe I'm attracted to her because she's forbidden. She has black hair and blue eyes, which, since she's been a widow, have been full of sadness and expectation. She's a woman who's waiting. She's raising her daughter, who is now thirteen years old, and continues teaching in a primary school. She's my type. Whenever I see her, she lowers her eyes as she says hello, smiling slightly. I must be her type too. But I prefer to think of her as she is rather than attempt anything irreparable. I'm honest with my wife too; I'm incapable of cheating on her. It's not that I wouldn't like to, but I have principles and I'm intent on respecting them. Najia is a vision, a smile, a dream in a corner of my memory. I think of her sweetly when Hlima's shouting sends me into a black pit with no exit. I spend a good deal of time at the bottom of this trap, where I'm reduced to the life of an animal. At these times a light goes on in my mind and I see Najia's radiant face. To go away with her, far away, to a foreign country, to go away without turning back, to run like teenagers on a deserted beach, accompanied by the music of Vivaldi; it would be cold and I'd cover her with my big Scottish wool sweater; she'd huddle against me, warm herself and lay her beautiful black hair on my shoulder... Ah! But it sounds like a movie for silly schoolgirls, an ad for perfume or a new car!

Haj Hamid knows how to be cruel. It's almost as if he reads my thoughts. Just as I'm beginning to hear Vivaldi, his harsh voice brings me back to the present. Through the glass door, he tells me that Mr. Sabbane has presented his application again. He emphasizes the name as if to convey that this time I have to sign. I tell him we're in no hurry and that we have all week to reevaluate his file and compare it with those of the other building contractors. In fact, I have given myself a timetable to think about it: one work week plus two weekends to make a decision.

On leaving the office I decide to walk. I'm in no rush to get home. I stop at the Alhambra bar and drink a beer, 15 dirhams, get my shoes polished while drinking it, a small luxury that costs me 5 dirhams, smoke two cigarettes, one of which is a Marlboro I buy from the kids who hang around the cafés. What will we eat tonight? Vegetable soup and a little Dutch cheese. It's light and not very expensive.

On my way home, I stop at the grocer. He presents me with the bill for the month of February: 1,852 DH. Is it worth looking at the breakdown? I know that the prices are doubled compared to the ordinary market. He sells things at higher prices and penalizes me because he gives me credit. I look at him and he smiles at me. I notice that the collar of his shirt is very dirty. Like all grocers, he's a Berber from the south, and spends all his time behind the cash register, eating and sleeping there. He's a pro at saving money. But is this a life? I give him a thousand dirhams and promise to pay off the rest soon. As I'm leaving I wonder: Does he have sex? He must never meet anyone since he never leaves his store. His wife and children are back in their village. At the end of a year, he'll spend two months with them and catch up. In the meantime, he masturbates in the filthy toilets in the back of the store.

MY WIFE IS IN A GOOD MOOD. WHAT LUCK. HER HAIR AND clothes are neat and she is speaking to me in a kind voice. Something must be wrong. She tells me about the neighbor, who is ordering an outfit from her for her brother's wedding and who even gave her a downpayment. That's it. Money makes her happy. She's right to feel that way. I smile and kiss her neck. Tonight we'll make love. Wassit is studying outdoors and Karima is sleeping. She hugs me and says, "Forgive me for all my tantrums, I can't help it. All I want is our children's happiness. Life is hard for honest people." I don't dare think of Najia anymore. And even if I were to put aside my scruples, I have nothing to offer her. She's a beautiful woman who needs lots of affection, but also to escape her life as a teacher, working day and night to make ends meet. I know that the indemnity money has been put in trust for her daughter.

I love Hlima, but I must admit that every time she reminds me how difficult our life is, it chips away at my affection. Najia seems nice, but I've learned that you only get to know people at unexpected moments, like during silences, or thanks to small details, in the way they react to insignificant events. Hlima, for example, hates lukewarm coffee. Sometimes I get up before her and prepare her breakfast. If she wakes up late, the coffee isn't hot anymore. That's when I hear her screaming and accusing me of having done it on purpose.

Hlima is a good mother. I'm present as a father but not very attentive. She has lots of patience with the kids. She knows how to talk to them and tell them stories to make them fall asleep. Meanwhile I'm calculating, adding and subtracting. From the twentieth of the month on, I rely on the grocer. It seems that loans with interest are forbidden in Islam, and yet the grocer prays and simply increases his prices to include the interest. A man who is broke after the twentieth of the month mustn't think about another woman. I have to erase the image of Najia from my mind. Whether in real life or at the movies, I've never seen a poor man succeed in seducing a beautiful woman with empty pockets, an overdrawn bank account, and a grocer who gives him credit. But thinking about it doesn't cost anything. I imagine things in order to air out my brain a bit. Far be it from me to ring her bell and propose a drive along the corniche. And yet it would be a good idea. Abbas would lend me his car and two or three hundred dirhams, and we'd take off like lovers to watch the white waves break along the shore. We'd eat kebabs and vanilla ice cream. I'd hold her next to me as we looked at the sea until she felt the beating of my heart. My heart would be beating quite hard, in fact, but more out of fear of running into someone from Hlima's family than out of feeling for Najia. I don't know. When I give up the idea, I feel better. It's extraordinary how easily people change. A minute ago I was filled with anxiety; all I had to do was chase this image from my mind to feel relieved, happy even.

I think all the time. I build things up and tear them down. I see things and I'm afraid. How do others do it? How does Sidi Larbi do it? He's never had this kind of problem. He can steal, corrupt, and swindle people and he's fine. Not only does he close his eyes and sleep in peace, but I'm sure he has many beautiful dreams that make for a wonderful sleep. But for me, just the thought of owing money to Abbas, my best friend, or to the grocer, my second banker, and I'm up all night. Perhaps if I crossed over, if I joined the ranks of the bastards, my scruples would vanish and I'd sleep like a log. I should try it. For them it comes naturally, whereas I need to force myself, to cut out a piece of my heart. I can't see myself intimating to a contractor that my commission is ten percent. He might lodge a complaint against me for corruption. How do the others do it? Why do I tremble and break into a cold sweat at the very idea of taking part in what is basically an everyday, common arrangement? Maybe I should take night classes. The thought of it makes me smile, because what would I use to pay for these night classes, if such things exist?

ABBAS IS A GOOD MAN WHO'S REMOVED FROM ALL OF THIS. He's rich and unassuming. His father left him property and buildings, and he manages the inheritances of his brothers and sisters. He's generous and discreet. The only time we fought was during the Gulf War. He participated in the rally in support of Saddam. It was claimed he was only supporting the Iraqi people, and that, in any case, Saddam was a symbol of resistance against the increasingly anti-Arab and anti-Muslim West. Abbas isn't a bad man but he allows himself to be easily persuaded by the vengeful slogans of a segment of the Arab press.

We met back in high school. He began studying law in Arabic and I left for France to study engineering. We were different, and we still are, but that doesn't prevent our friendship from being solid. After the Gulf War business, we tacitly decided not to talk politics anymore. The other day, he came to see me and told me I was right about Saddam. He had just read a United Nations document on the toxic gases the Iraqi Secret Service dropped on Halabjah, a village inhabited by Kurds, who were all killed in their sleep. I also reminded him of what Saddam's enemy, the Syrian Hafiz al Asad, by far the more intelligent of the two, did in Hamah.

We agree on one point: the Arab peoples, in particular those in the Middle East, have no luck. On top of this, the West punishes them because their leaders are dictators.

"Politics is for do-nothings and parasites," my grocer tells me. The only politics he practices are those of credit and inflated prices. Add to that his mania for praying in the back of the store without performing his ablutions.

Abbas is often forced to corrupt elements within the government. He doesn't do it directly; his chauffeur is good at it, he's a clever, loyal man. He has common sense: "You have someone who doesn't pay his rent? You sue him. If you go through the normal channels it can take four or five years. If you follow the parallel route, it's settled in a matter of months. And this is the only road that leads anywhere. Believe me, it's neither bad nor dishonest. It's reasonable, realistic. You bridge the gaps in the state. You're not doing anything wrong. I'm all for law and order. But when everyone passes through the hidden door and everything is handled in the corridors, it would be suicidal to do otherwise. The country works well this way. Do we have the wherewithal to give up this system? I don't think so. And people have gotten used to it. Before even taking the normal route of going to pick up a document, for example—which is simple—they start by looking for someone to intervene." Abbas also claims to be realistic. He considers it a contribution to national solidarity. Corruption is a supplementary tax in disguise. Everyone goes along with it, and people like me, who resist, will soon have to be kept on a preserve, next to the endangered species. Personally, I'll be proud to be on this preserve.

How much longer will my pride last? Will this pride give my eldest the means to continue his studies, will it pay for medicine for my youngest, who's asthmatic, will it enable me to take my little family on vacation?

Sometimes I think of taking a second job. I could do the bookkeeping for a company, working at night at their office or at home. I'll talk to Abbas about it. He doesn't need a bookkeeper since he keeps his books himself, but he could introduce me to some of his friends. He likes to be helpful. He's happy to do it, but it's a matter of finding a company that doesn't already have someone.

I don't know why, but people like me are condemned to moving through a tunnel. I have no way out. All I have to do is choose a path and it grows hollow and turns into a tunnel, at the end of which there is often a pit. It's a nightmare I have frequently. I'm walking down the street, alone, in broad daylight. Suddenly I find a wallet full of money on the ground. I bend down to pick it up, the street also bends, becomes a slope, and the wallet slides away, then the sky grows dark, the more I walk the longer the slope becomes, I can't keep my balance anymore, I slip and end up several yards underground, in a corridor full of murky water. I advance like a blind man and go on like this forever, until Hlima wakes me up because my panting is disturbing her. She thinks it's my own fault that I sleep so badly. I think too much. I place too much emphasis on details, I insist that each thing be in its place. It's true that I think, I even think a lot. Not that I'm philosophical. I imagine, placing stone upon stone. I examine everything, I analyze the consequences of each act, of each fact. Perhaps I'm obsessive. That's what my wife accuses me of. I read into the future. I'm not psychic but I foresee what will happen if I do one thing or another. I calculate. In the depths of my tunnel, I never stop calculating. My father was like me: economical out of necessity, forced to be careful. We all had enough to eat, but just barely. No luxuries, nothing extravagant, everything in moderation. He refused to live on credit like most people. When he died, I went to the bank with my brother to close his account. We were horrified to find that the entire fortune of this man who had started working at the age of fourteen amounted to a few thousand dirhams. That he had worked so hard for almost seventy years to arrive at this ridiculous sum made us angry. At that point I realized he had done what he had to: I had thought he was cheap, because he was constantly haggling, but in fact he was forced to be economical. Now I regret having been disrespectful, having accused him of stinginess. Poverty is not always a good adviser. It pushes people to break the law, steal, swindle and lie. Not him. He was proud of his dignity; he was a poor man but a fine, dedicated worker. He didn't like lazy people or those who play around. He would say that life was brutal, pitiless, cruel, but also beautiful and wonderful. "I'm more familiar with its first aspect," he would add with a smile. I resemble him, but do I have his strength and courage? One day, during one of our fights, Hlima screamed at me, "You're like your father!" Coming from her it was an insult. She didn't like him much. The feeling was mutual. He said out loud what he thought of the underhanded ways of her family, more worried about appearances, about luxury and money, than about people's inner qualities. He wasn't easy on them, and, more than that—which was very disturbing for us—he denounced their hypocrisy. No one could silence him. He knew the price of everything and counted his pennies. He wasn't ashamed to do it. He was never easy with money. I'm like him. He used to say it's hard to get rich if you're honest. He protested about paying his taxes because he couldn't see where the money went. What's more, he gave ten percent of his income to the poor, in keeping with Koranic law. The *zakat* was sacred to him. But when a beggar who was in good health would ask for the *zakat*, he'd refused to give it: "You're healthy, you have arms, you could work…" he'd tell him. "A vigorous man like you should be ashamed to ask for alms!"

I MUST WRITE THE MUNICIPALITY TO TELL THEM HOW I suffer taking the bus every morning. The City Council could buy more buses. That's what they were elected for, among other things. But rumor has it these people couldn't care less about public transportation, they get around in government cars and don't even pay for gas. Anyway, they're busy making deals and have neither the time nor the desire to tend to the masses. It wouldn't do any good to write, unless the letter were published on the front page of a foreign newspaper. That would get them moving. Often you have to work through a foreign country to change things. Obviously if *Le Monde* were to publish an exposé on daily life here, and if the journalist were to live under our real conditions, the leaders would be extremely upset. Alas, we have to wait for Casablanca to become a megalopolis like Cairo or New Delhi before we react. The poor citizen has no rights. I am a poor citizen so I know what I'm talking about. The advantage I have over the people at the municipality is that I know the real situation and I know what I'm talking about.

Listen, a voice inside me is murmuring: "You're a poor citizen, but you don't have to be one. Your situation is in your hands. Don't spend your life taking that stinking bus—one day it's going to drop you in a common grave! Wake up. Think of your children's future. What you call corruption is in fact only a subtle way of recouping what's yours. Everyone gets by. Be flexible, old pal. Flexibility is what life's all about. Go ahead, get on your bus, let yourself be crushed, shoved, your nose in the face of this man who doesn't brush his teeth because he doesn't have any and whose breath is pretty bad, let yourself be manhandled by this messenger who forgot to wash and who'll give you his fleas, you, an official at the Ministry of Development. When you get off this bus, your only suit is all wrinkled, you smell bad, and your feet hurt because they were stepped on and you couldn't even shout. You're pitiful! Even your father wouldn't have let you take this sorry bus; it pollutes the city and may very well tip over one day under the weight of these poor souls who have no choice. You at least could change your situation. You could give your wife and children a more decent, respectable, flexible life. Yes, my friend, flexibility, flexibility... and you'll see that all the rest will follow. You ask me what the rest is? You're right. It's vague. Let's imagine. It's easy for you to imagine, it's your specialty. You spend your life imagining things. So let's take it one step at a time. First, you buy a car, maybe not new, but a good used one. You'll go to Tangier and you'll find lots of foreign cars there belonging to immigrants. You'll buy a Mercedes 240 diesel; that's one big problem solved. Once you have the car, you'll move. To a house, say. This isn't so easy, but for the meantime you'll rent one. One of your clients will have a house to rent. All you have to do is put the word out. Once you have the house, you furnish it. Hlima can take care of that. And then you have to think about entertaining. If you don't entertain your clients at home, you won't be able to get ahead in your business dealings. That's clear. Next, you have to dress better. Appearances are everything. If you're poor, it's because you look like a poor man. You can tell a rich man right away. It's not a matter of showing off your wealth, but there are certain unmistakable signs. You have to go out, go to restaurants from time to time, so that you are seen dining with important people, so that everyone knows you're a man who doesn't count his pennies. It's important to leave a big tip for the waiter; that makes you seem rich and generous at the same time. You also have to go to the mosque, say, on Fridays. You'll make an effort, you'll put aside your secularity and your atheism and you'll play the game. That's society. An endless game. You have to know how to maneuver, to move from one place to another, to overcome obstacles, to circumvent difficulties, to get rid of useless things, like scruples and a guilty conscience..."

THE TIRELESS VOICE TALKS, TALKS, RUNS THROUGH MY blood, following its rhythm, while I, at times attentive, at times deaf to it, close my eyes in this bus that is barreling down a road that must be the roof of the world; I can barely manage to look out the window and see only a string of red, green, and yellow meadows. And here I am, floating above this fray of grass and flowers, forgetting that the man crushing my chest is obese and that his sweat is suffocating. The voice gets under my skin, it circulates like a foreign body in my intestines, runs everywhere, hovers over me, then falls back to the base of my throat. I still hear it even if I plug my ears. "So, change the world!" I say to myself. And it answers me, "No, change your life." I hear it shout and emphasize "Your life" as if I were deaf, then it becomes unpleasant and even insulting: "Change the world! He thinks he's a poet, a revolutionary, a hero. Poor guy! It's a matter of changing your pathetic little life, of making it a little less pathetic, that's all. You're not going to change the world, and the world couldn't care less about your miserable little life, which isn't worth two cents. Do you know that in the United States your life isn't worth a dollar? If someone wanted to kill you, he'd hire a hit man for a dollar, but if he had to eliminate Haj Hamid, your assistant, your subordinate, he'd offer several thousand dollars. Because Haj Hamid is more important than you. He lives better and supports other people. You can't even support your children, and you're the head of an office where your assistant's scorn for you is building up like the mildew on the wall of the old house in the medina, where your poor mother is dying in the cold and damp. It'll be partly your fault when she dies. Nonassistance to a person in danger. Your mother deserves to live in a nice, comfortable house, with maids, a cook, a car, and a chauffeur. Your father left her nothing. But you, you could have a little more imagination and make yourself useful to your nearest and dearest, your mother first, your children next, and finally your wife. As for you, you've gotten used to simple living and you can continue to live simply, it won't bother anyone. Do you know something? I'm embarrassed to be your voice. I suffer every time you use me. You use me pointlessly. At least take me to do your business, to finalize contracts, to discuss interesting projects, to travel to Japan, yes, I dream of no longer belonging to you and of finding myself inside a real man, one who is rich and respected. No one even says hello to you, you're so poor. You don't exist. No one sees you anymore. You arrive at the office and the *chaouch* wonders if you're not a beggar come to ask for a little money. Have you seen yourself? Do you realize what you look like? The way you walk with your head down, the way you skirt the walls. Tell me how you managed to seduce Hlima. How could she have married you? She deserves better than you and you know it, you tell yourself that all the time. And to think that you dream of seducing the beautiful Najia. Don't you realize she's more demanding than Hlima, and that she has more than one trick up her sleeve? In fact, it might be a good idea to give it a go. Maybe you'd realize that flexibility is the only solution you have left. I'm shutting up. I'm leaving. I'm getting out from under your conscience, which must weigh a ton or more. It's crushing me, it's suffocating me, it's hurting me. Do you realize, I've become the enemy of your conscience. It's taking up all the room. One day it'll suffocate you. I'm getting out of here. Farewell, my friend. I'm leaving you the other one, the hard, dry voice, the accomplice of your conscience. They were made for each other."

The bus brakes suddenly. Some of the passengers have fallen on top of those in front. Some are pressed up against the windshield. They insult the hapless driver, who says he's cursed to work for this company. "At least you're working!" a man answers him. "Thank God at least." "God has nothing to do with it!" cries a crotchety old man, his eyes shining. A bearded man shouts: *"Allah Akbar! Allah Akbar!* You'll all go to hell!" The bus has come to a halt. A crowd has already gathered around the little fruit cart drawn by a tired donkey. Everything has tipped over. The owner, an old man who's as tired as the donkey, apparently hasn't been hurt. He bends over to pick up his oranges and bananas. People help him. "It's nothing," he says, "I don't need the police or an ambulance." He's afraid. He wants to run away. A police officer arrives. "Don't touch anything. Show me your papers." "They're at home." "I don't believe you. Follow us to the station." People intervene. The old man fills a bag with fruit and holds it out to the officer, who says, "You think you can buy me off with that? Come on, we're going to the station!" The bus starts up again. Everyone has an opinion. I hear all sorts of things. My obese neighbor thinks that a hundred dirhams will get the old man released. "You mean a hundred dirhams per officer," another answers him. "That'll be about a thousand dirhams, and that's if they're nice." I too want to put in a word, in defense of the police. After all, we have no proof. The officers did their work. Why suspect them of corruption in advance? That's what the other voice tells me, the good, humane, just voice. Then it starts reproaching me for listening to the voice of evil: "You're forty years old, you're an honest worker, you struggle to remain a man of integrity and dignity, and here you are threatening to soften. I feel it. There are telltale signs. Why else did you go see the real estate agent yesterday to find out about houses for rent? Just getting information, you say! And the other day, why did you stop in front of the Mercedes garage? To feast my eyes, you say. I'd like to believe you. You can't lie to me. I know what you think. That's what I'm here for, after all. I stick to your skin and invade your sleep, I'm responsible for your insomnia. I resist all your sleeping pills—you did well to stop taking them. I'm here to remind you of the law, of principles, of duty and righteousness. It's not an easy job; my powers are limited. What can I do if you decide to jump ship, if you accept compromises and gradually lose your virtue and your standards? True, I'll prevent you from sleeping, but not for long; I'll call on the good sense and intelligence of your youngest daughter. Karima will never allow you to lose your honor so stupidly. She's your guilty conscience. She's the one who'll replace me when you lose your reason. I love Karima. At twelve, she's well beyond her years. Her maturity is remarkable. It's astounding how she manages to intimidate her mother with glances and silences. Think of her before you get entangled in something you don't know the half of."

ON MY WAY OFF THE BUS, I REALIZE THAT THE RIGHT pocket of my jacket is torn. I can't go to the office like this. Better to take the jacket off and come in looking casual, sporty. People won't understand, though; it's winter. So what. I have the right to carry my jacket on my arm. What will the *chaouch* say? He really gets to me. This guy, a peasant, a former member of the auxiliaries, once tried to bribe me. One day, on the eve of Aïd, he offered me a lamb. I refused it. He was offended, but his gesture was in no way innocent. Later, I learned that he was illegally selling his services, obtaining documents and appointments for people. He has two wives, eight children, and a motorbike. One day he had the nerve to offer me a ride home on his bike. I have nothing against the working classes, but this errand boy clearly wanted to humiliate me.

I walk through the door and by chance my enemy the *chaouch* isn't in. Haj Hamid hasn't arrived yet. There's a needle and thread in my drawer. I have a hard time threading the needle; my sight is going. How annoying. My hands are shaking. Finally I get it. I sew, feeling ridiculous. If Haj Hamid walks in on me, I'll really be embarrassed. He'll make fun of me and he'll be right. I darn my own socks; Hlima refuses to do it. It's degrading. She'll only mend the children's clothing. What a wretched picture: a forty-year-old professional with a college degree, married, with two children, sits behind his desk mending the torn pocket of his jacket! Seen from the outside, it's pitiful and amusing. Before, the *chaouch* used to bring me a glass of mint tea. It was a tradition. For some time now, he's been forgetting. Each time, I have to call him and ask for it. I take advantage of Haj Hamid's absence to give Najia a call. I'm waking her; just my luck. Her voice is distant. I mutter some excuse and say it was a mistake. She sleeps alone. Her mother divides her time between her and her younger sister. It would be better to meet her by chance; I'll arrange the chance. All I have to do is go past her school when it lets out. I could offer to accompany her home and we'll go part of the way together. If the weather is nice we'll walk, perhaps stopping at the Renaissance pastry shop to eat a few *cornes de gazelle*. She's slim. She must not overindulge in sweets.

Haj Hamid comes in and puts Mr. Sabbane's folder on my desk, telling me, as if I were his subordinate, that I must resolve this problem very quickly. I open the folder, study the plans and blueprints. I get up and pace around the office. I go to the window, smoke a cigarette, and witness a fight between two motorcyclists. It's strange, suddenly people seem more aggressive. An argument can flare up over nothing. Haj Hamid gets up too, alerted by the sound of insults, then sits back down.

"It's the drought," he says, philosophically.

"You mean people are fighting because it's not raining?"

"Of course. The bluer the sky, the emptier the pockets. It's only normal. So what have you decided about Mr. Sabbane?"

"He has to participate in the bidding, like everyone else."

"But of course he'll participate. That's a formality, as you know, and we're here to ensure that the formalities go smoothly. Study the folder carefully. I have a doctor's appointment, so I'll be gone for an hour. I'm having back trouble. It seems it's the illness of intellectuals. I'll see you later. Don't miss a page of that folder."

I FLIP THROUGH IT. I DON'T UNDERSTAND WHY HAJ HAMID insists I study it. Between two files is a fairly thick envelope with nothing marked on it. A white envelope. It could be for anyone. I know what's in it but I open it anyway. Two stacks of one-hundred- and two-hundred-dirham bills. I count them. The bills are new. I count them again. I hear a noise in the corridor and put them back in the envelope. I'm shaking. I've never held so many bills in my hands. I leave the envelope where it is and pretend to read the pages. I'm reading and thinking of the twenty thousand dirhams. I tell myself this could be a start. In a few minutes I could earn four times my monthly salary. If I repeat this operation in two weeks' time, I'll be rich. I close the folder and fall into a daydream. I realize that the change will be abrupt. Everyone will suspect something. My wife will be delighted, but her mother won't miss the chance to remind me that my virtue is not what it was.

I close the folder and put a rubber band around it. I push it far away from me and stare at it. Its thickness taunts me. Yes, this is how it starts. A white or gray envelope with no name on it. It's like finding a wallet on the street. Ultimately, you take what's inside and throw the wallet in the garbage. I'm tempted to empty the envelope. If I do that, there'll be no going back. The gears will go into motion. My life will be transformed. There'll be a "before" and an "after" the envelope. I get up, smoke a cigarette, and look out the window. I see a woman sitting on a balcony, coating her loose hair with henna. It's an erotic image. I think of her, not as she is now but after her bath; I can almost smell the scent of henna, the scent of her skin. On the balcony above, a young girl, probably the maid, is hanging out laundry. On the terrace of the little house wedged between two buildings, a child is playing with kittens while his mother is putting out black olives to dry.

DOWN BELOW, THE LINE AT THE BUS STOP IS GROWING. It's chaos. When the bus pulls up, a cloud of black smoke spurts from the exhaust pipe. People hold their noses. The nearby doughnut man is up in arms. Everything smells like diesel fuel. The butt of my cigarette burns my fingers. I return to my desk and again the file intrudes. All I can see on the desk is Mr. Sabbane's file. It's grown, its dimensions are abnormal. I rub my eyes, I'm hallucinating. My guilty conscience is affecting my vision. I decide to postpone the examination of this sensitive file until later. That's what I tell Haj Hamid, who repeats the word *sensitive* several times, smiling. He thinks it's the beginning of a complicity between us. He gets up and offers to get me a coffee or something else to drink. In his mind we're going to celebrate our new partnership. He's wrong. I think he's wrong. I'm not sure. I'm not sure about anything. I'm imagining things. He comes back with a coffee and a Coke. I take the coffee. He raises his bottle and motions as if to drink to my health. "Cheers," he says. How ridiculous, to offer a toast with a bottle of Coke and a cup of coffee! There's something absurd about this situation. He approaches and takes me by the shoulder:

"Life isn't always kind. You have to know how to go with the flow. If not, you suffocate. There are turning points where everyone wins, and it's all done with flexibility. I'm going to give you the address of a friend who brings designer suits back from France. Tell him I sent you and he'll give you a good price. It's all done in his apartment. He's the one who dresses me, and our director likes him a lot too. You don't have to pay him right away. Pick out a nice suit, anything but gray, and relax."

I feel flexibility overtaking me. I compare it to a downy sofa into which your body gently sinks. I let myself go, my head back, I no longer see the world as it is, no longer feel my muscles, I am elsewhere, on a sailboat in the Mediterranean, my eyes closed, my face lightly caressed by the breeze; I am happy. The telephone rings. It's the director speaking in a calm voice. This must be the voice of complicity. He tells me about a dinner at his house with a few friends, including Mr. Sabbane. Things are clear. But what he doesn't know is that I haven't decided anything yet. My wife calls. Karima is having another asthma attack and I should buy some Ventoline. But the best thing for her would be a change of climate. I could send her to my mother's, in Fez, but the house is damp. The air in Marrakech would be more suitable for Karima and we have a cousin there, but I don't dare ask him to put her up for a while. Like my father, I don't like to owe anything. Yet this cousin sometimes turns up at our house unannounced and sleeps in the children's room.

When Karima has an asthma attack, I suffer and hate myself for not being able to do something to relieve her. It's true that with a little money we could spare her some of these bouts. The doctor says it will straighten itself out as she gets older.

I'm alone in the office again. I take the phone off the hook to have some quiet time to think. I wonder if others have such a difficult time, if their stomachs get tied up in knots, if their throats get dry and their hands shake. I don't know any more whether I'm trembling because of the cigarette or the situation. I stand up, stretch out my right arm, and place a sheet of paper on the back of my hand in order to get a better sense of how bad it is. Our old gymnastics teacher taught us to measure the condition of our bodies this way. I sit back down and look at the folder. This time, my father's face slowly comes into focus. I can't tell if he's encouraging or disapproving. His expression is ambiguous. Ordinarily he always condemned these practices. Perhaps, wherever he is, he has learned flexibility. Others call it "an understanding." For the moment, I'm not there yet. I'm barely at the height of my guilty conscience. I'm negotiating with it. I air my grievances, paint an alarming picture so that it will authorize a small escapade, a slight lapse. I hear the other voice say: "Twenty thousand smackers, you call that a slight lapse? Let's say it's a major blemish on your record, an enormous exception to the rule..."

I remember when my office at the Ministry of Development was recruiting personnel. I received a rather original application letter. Written in French, probably with a goose feather, it was soliciting work as if we lived in another century:

*May God enlarge your dwelling and fill it with kindness and the laughter of children!*

*May God open the paths of light and fortune to you!*

*May your heart remain clean, pure, clear of shadow and disorder!*

*May your eyes remain open and your hearing intact, for what I am about to tell you is none other than the story of an innocent man taken in by gold-plated words. I shall not bore you. Know that my father was a pillar of the city and that our house was always open, with its spacious courtyards where a horse freely roamed. Know that misfortune exists, that illwill and hypocrisy are more commonplace than you think. Ingratitude too is very widespread. Here I am today in your hands, at the mercy of your good judgment, of your kindness. Here I am as free as our horse in the courtyard, but of what use is freedom if it is not exercised in work? All this to appeal to your great generosity for a position in your fine office at the Ministry of Development.*

*May God grant that this letter reach you neither before your morning coffee, nor after an annoyance, nor during a moment of rest. It must arrive at the right moment, but how shall I know? I shall know by your response, which I hope will be favorable and swift.*

*Your present and future servant...*

As I was folding this letter, I noticed some writing—light, in pencil, at the bottom of the page on the left margin. The writing was so small I had a hard time reading it: *If you hire me, I'll give you one thousand dirhams. It will remain our secret!*

It was a murmur, a whisper, something barely said, thus barely visible, erasable since it was written in pencil.

I wanted to laugh. I took an eraser, wiped out the whisper and gave the file to the personnel director. I never knew whether this man was hired or not.

A THOUSAND DIRHAMS! AT THE TIME IT WAS A LOT OF money, at least the monthly salary of a teacher. I had spoken to my wife about it, who had laughed and hadn't understood why I didn't respond personally to the proposition.

I AM STILL ALONE IN THE OFFICE. MY ASSISTANT HASN'T returned yet. Perhaps he is leaving me alone on purpose so I can decide. I pick up the envelope again and try to weigh it in my hands. I put it in the inside pocket of my jacket. You can see I'm carrying something bulky. It could be a fat wallet or a bundle of letters. Love letters, for example. I have always been fascinated by the image of love letters tied up with a ribbon and returned to their sender. Did I write Hlima love letters? I don't remember. But Najia's the one I want to write to. I stand up, walk, and feel different. I'm a rich man. A question crosses my mind: Is the twenty thousand for me alone or do I have to share it? I think that the second hypothesis is more plausible. If I do share it, with whom should it be? With Haj Hamid, the boss, or the *chaouch*?

The telephone rings. It's the boss asking where Mr. Sabbane's folder is. I tell him I'm studying it. He hangs up. I feel I'm being pressured. I imagine the worst: being caught red-handed accepting a bribe. I'm arrested, humiliated, thrown to the mercy of my in-laws, my children deprived of the little I can provide for them. What a nightmare! Someone knocks on the door. The *chaouch* brings me a glass of tea and asks for news of my children. It's as if someone alerted him. I thank him, take a sip of tea, remove the packet of money from my pocket, and divide it into two yellowish envelopes which I lock in the right-hand drawer. I sign all the documents without even reading them and ring the buzzer. The *chaouch* comes quickly. I hand him the folder and ask him to take it to the registration office. I heave a great sigh of relief. It was simple, fast, and uneventful. I've been crazy to burden myself with so many scruples. I've taken the first step. I am no longer the same, I'm becoming a better man. I open one of the two envelopes and pull out two blue two-hundred-dirham notes. They're brand-new, all clean and still smelling of the printing press. I lock the drawer again and leave my office. It's lunchtime. I take a taxi and tell the driver: restaurant La Mer, in Aïn Diab. I've always dreamed of eating seafood in this restaurant. Once our director invited us there to celebrate his birthday. I decide to treat myself to two hours of happiness. It's selfish, but why not?

I sit facing the sea. It's a beautiful day, the waves tall and white. I love hearing the sound they make crashing against the cliff. I call the waiter and ask for cigarettes first, Gitanes, unfiltered, then I order. Despite my small fortune, I read the menu from right to left, from the price to the dish. I make a rapid calculation. A shrimp appetizer, sole meunière, and a crème brûlée… 279 DH, plus a half-bottle of Cabernet and a bottle of Oulmès mineral water; the whole thing shouldn't come to more than 300 DH.

I savor every instant. I relax, forget my problems, put aside anything that might spoil these two hours of freedom and pleasure for me. I think of Najia, of her body. For the first time I undress her and discover her firm breasts, her flat stomach and her well rounded buttocks. At thirty-eight or thirty-nine, she is still very beautiful. It must be the wine: I dare to imagine what I have refused to let myself imagine before. I should drink from time to time, I'm sure it would help me face difficult situations. After a wonderful meal with plenty to drink, I pay the check, leave a tip, and request a taxi. I'm treated like a VIP, like a boss. It's nice. I won't tell anyone about this escapade. I feel light and full at the same time. I ask the taxi driver to go slowly. I don't feel like returning to the office so soon; I have to make the moment last. He suggests a ride along the corniche. I accept. People are sunning themselves in front of cafés on this early spring day. They're happy, even though the sky is still blue. I think again about the rain that has forgotten us this year and become optimistic, believing the country will pull through. I identify with the country and tell myself that if I come out okay, it too will be saved.

At the office, Haj Hamid welcomes me with a big smile. He gets up and comes toward me, his hand extended. I greet him. He waits, then, to convey what he's after, locks the door. I open the drawer and hand him his envelope. He slips it into his briefcase and leaves the office, saying "See you tomorrow!" He's off to stash his money. He must have a safe at the bank. I should do the same. If I go from being a poor man to a rich man too suddenly, I'll be noticed right away. I have to go slowly. Not say anything to Hlima. I'll hide the money in the bookcase. I'll put it in a big book, say Jean-Paul Sartre's *Being and Nothingness*, which I bought at the flea market in the medina. That way if I reverse the title, and go from nothingness to being, the book will in a sense be about me. No one would think to read this huge tome. I like what he writes about the gaze. At a certain moment, I experience what Sartre says about the waiter in the café. I am going through the daily and quasi-mechanical motions of an office worker without imagination and without surprises. I think that from now on things will change. I take out a brand-new pad of paper and on the first page jot down a few decisions:

~ *From now on, I am going to change.* I stop and ask myself: "How can a forty-year-old man still change? You know it's impossible. You change when you're young, when you're searching for yourself, you don't change at this age." Let's just say that it's a resolution I'm making, we'll see what happens later. But change what? My way of walking, first of all. I must walk with my head held high, my back straight, and my hands swinging. If I manage to change this aspect of myself, I'll have accomplished something.

~ *In order to walk naturally, you have to be at ease in your clothing; therefore I must change my style of dress. I'll wear baggy suits and good shoes. I've often read in magazines that a man's elegance begins with his shoes. Stop being afraid to wear colors.*

~ *I am also going to stop smoking. I'll wait for Ramadan to stop poisoning my lungs.*

~ *I will no longer watch television. Instead I'll read or listen to music. (Buy a stereo.)*

~ *I will stop spending weekends at home. I'll take my family to the beach or the mountains. You have to live a little. (Buy a car, probably a used one.)*

~ *Eat slowly. (Stop eating between meals.)*

~ *Take up a sport. (Calisthenics or bicycling.)*

~ *Keep a diary. (Buy a safe and hide it, along with the money that will fall from the sky.)*

~ *As for Najia, I must have a serious talk with her soon.*

I buy a bouquet of flowers which I plan to leave at Najia's. If no one is home, I'll give it to Hlima. She might ask me embarrassing questions. I don't ordinarily bring flowers home. I'll tell her that the boss gave us a bonus and that I'm celebrating.

I feel like a different man. I'm expecting my other voice to intervene at any moment. Strangely enough, it doesn't speak up. I have placed my signature on a document that will allow a man to do his work. I haven't stolen, I haven't taken anything from anyone. I have simply facilitated an action. With ten thousand dirhams, I'll breathe a little easier. I'll settle up with the grocer. Better still, on Sunday, I'll go to the wholesale market and stock up for several weeks. I'll put everything in a Toyota taxi and the days of credit with interest from the grocer who doesn't even wash will be over. I'll tell my wife it's the bonus money and hope she won't ask too many questions.

One of my main problems in life is that I don't know how to lie. I've learned, over time, to lie by omission, which is a form of cowardice. I say nothing. The silence creeps along, masked by forgetfulness. My wife knows it. She discovers whatever I try to hide. All you have to do is stare at me for a second and I lose my cool. When I get home, she'll see that something has changed; she'll besiege me, throw questions at me from every angle. I'll stay quiet and won't move. Unless I split the money with her, for the sake of having some peace.

If she could read my mind, at night, when she's sleeping beside me, she would strangle me. I imagine myself a widower, the children already on their own. I imagine Najia in my arms, in my life. I put aside any unpleasant thoughts about Najia: sick, for instance, or angry, unkempt and neglected, letting herself go. Often wives make no effort to be pretty at home; they dress any which way and barely comb their hair. The husband no longer has to be seduced.

Hlima isn't home yet. Karima tells me that she's at her mother's. Generally when she spends time with her mother, she comes back charged up, ready for battle. I take advantage of her absence to hide the money in *Being and Nothingness*, take a shower, and look over my daughter's homework. The mathematics they teach them in school is different from what I learned. I keep Karima company as she struggles with formulas. I put my hand on her shoulder. She looks up at me as if she needs something and I notice great sadness in her eyes. My eyes fill with tears.

"Why is mother mad at you and us so often?" she asks me. "She says it's your fault we're poor. Is that true?"

I ask her if she needs something in particular. Her face lights up.

"Yes, I'd like to go on a trip with you! It's my dream. I know we don't have enough money to do what other people do. But one day, if you make a lot of money, you'll come wake me and take me to Tangier to see where the two oceans meet."

"I'd like to take a trip with you, too. I promise that one day I'll come take you to the land of your dreams."

HLIMA COMES IN, FURIOUS. AS SOON AS SHE SEES THE bouquet of flowers, she lowers her voice and asks if we have company. Karima turns toward her and signals in my direction with her eyes.

"So you forget to buy bread and milk. Instead, you bring us flowers. That's a new one! What's this all about?"

For once I decide to tell the truth:

"I bought these flowers for a lady who is distinguished and kind. She wasn't home so I brought them here."

"So that's it! What woman would want a penniless man like you? She'd have to be crazy or depraved. We have some in the neighborhood, in fact. You have plenty to choose from, starting with your cousin. She's so lonely she'd be happy with a failure like you. Go ahead, try, tell me about it afterwards."

Without getting excited, without saying a word, I go to the bookshelf, take down *Thus Spake Zarathustra* and *Being and Nothingness*, and put them in a plastic bag; I bend over Karima, kiss her, and leave without slamming the door. Outside, the air is mild. I pull out a Gitanes and light it. I feel carefree, even happy. My ears are still ringing with Hlima's voice. I head toward Najia's house and press the buzzer. She opens the door herself. Surprised, she invites me in and asks if everything's okay.

"No. Things are not okay, but I need to talk to you. I must be disturbing you."

"You're not disturbing me. I just finished correcting my students' assignments. My daughter is sleeping and my mother left a week ago to visit her older brother."

She seats me in the living room. On the main wall is her wedding photo. She looks tired while her husband is smiling. It's as if she knows that fate will strike them. Why else would she look so on edge? She brings me orange juice, then, after a silence, asks me:

"Is it because of Hlima? I saw her the other day at the *hammam*. She wasn't very friendly. I assumed she must be unhappy."

"Yes, she is."

"What are you going to do now?"

"For the moment, I'd like to rest a bit."

"Did anyone see you come in?"

"No, I don't think so. "

"The reason I ask is because people are vicious. They watch me and say bad things about me. It's hard to be a single woman in this country. Sometimes I feel like having a drink and smoking a cigarette outside a café by the ocean. If I were to do it, people would take me for a whore. So I go home and take care of my daughter. At night I'm cold. Loneliness makes you cold. No matter how many blankets I wrap myself in, my limbs feel frozen. A body filled with cold ends up dying. Sometimes, when she has nightmares, my daughter sleeps snuggled up against me. Her little body warms me... Why am I telling you all this? Even though we're cousins we hardly know each other, but I see my reflection in sad faces; I find something familiar, a resonance. Right now, I feel you're very close to me, that I know how you feel. You're like a mirror."

I take her hands and warm them, rubbing them against my own. She cries in silence, then slowly lays her head on my shoulder.

It's been some time since I've had such a strong and beautiful emotion. I'm afraid I'll spoil everything if I start talking again. I hold her against me and kiss her cheeks, which are wet with tears.

WE SPEND THE NIGHT ON THE SOFA. I SLEEP VERY LITTLE. Her body, which grows more and more relaxed, is next to mine. From time to time, a shiver runs through her. At dawn I rise and go to the office. I put my two books on her bookshelf and tiptoe out of the living room.

Hlima is waiting for me at the entrance to the Ministry of Development, disheveled from lack of sleep. She didn't think I was capable of taking action. She comes toward me, looking pitiful.

"Where were you?"

"It's none of your business."

A friend taught me to be indifferent. It seems it's often an effective approach. I keep walking. She follows me and begins shouting. Since I am already out of sight, people don't know who she's yelling at. From the window I see her walking away like a beggar.

THREE FOLDERS HAVE BEEN PLACED ON MY DESK IN MY absence. They are marked *Confidential*, with *Very Urgent* added by hand.

I have the impression that yesterday is very far away. In one fell swoop, I became a corrupt man, discovered luxury, and almost cheated on my wife. So much upheaval in such a short period of time! It's enough to lose your balance. In fact, I do feel dizzy. I almost fell before when I went to smoke by the open window. I may be sick. The other day on the radio I heard a doctor say, matter-of-factly, that after the age of forty you have to have an anal exam to check your prostate. From this age on, you have to make some changes. Fine, I started yesterday. I'm turning over a new leaf, I'm forgetting the past and placing great stock in the future, since everything will be facilitated by money. For the moment, I don't know what to do. To whom should I give priority? To myself or my children? As usual, I will let events guide me, but I will nonetheless watch out for my children's well-being. I'll stop by the house tonight to change clothes and look over Karima's homework. Then I'll slip away. I'll go to Najia's. This time I'll talk to her about the future, our future.

I open one of the three folders at random. I begin by look- ing for the thick envelope. There is none. Neither of the two other files has one either. It may be an oversight, or else they're coming later. I wait for Haj Hamid to arrive; he's an expert, he'll tell me what to do. I wonder if I should talk to him directly or let him come to me. He takes a cut, after all, and he's accustomed to dealing with these matters. I leave everything as is, pull out the large account book and read a few pages mechanically.

The *chaouch*, all smiles, tells me that Mr. Sabbane would like to see me. Suddenly I'm afraid. What does he want from me? Did he perhaps change his mind? Does he want a cut too?... That would be too much... Anything is possible once you get caught in the works. I tell him to wait a moment. I would like my assistant to be present. If there's a problem, he'll know better than I how to deal with it. I have always said that Haj Hamid is more Moroccan than I am. He knows how to talk, he knows the art of enveloping things in poetic and some-times religious formulas that make those he's talking to giddy. He knows verses of Chawki and Omar Khayyám by heart, hadiths of the Prophet, city and country proverbs. As they say in Arabic, "his tongue is a blade."

The door opens. Haj Hamid and Mr. Sabbane enter, hand in hand. Haj Hamid introduces us. I mutter a few words to be polite and explain that we already know one another. The *chaouch* brings in a platter of tea and coffee. I notice a plate of croissants and *cornes de gazelle*. It's the first time the office has been so generous. They're relaxed. I'm a nervous wreck. I'm sweating, uttering nonsense. I don't dare look this man in the eye. I'm not my usual self. What harm is there in having a cup of coffee with one of the contractors? And what harm is there even in having taken the envelope? I listen to their discussion, thinking of other things.

"The sky is stingy this year!"

"If it doesn't rain, there'll be more and more beggars..."

"Lamb will flood the market and its price will be halved..."

"How is it that it's raining in Spain and not here?"

"We have a police commissioner who rapes hundreds of girls and women in his bachelor flat, films them, and sends the cassettes to Europe... God is punishing us."

"Ah, that commissioner is a monster. I wonder what his lawyers will plead? Insanity?"

I cough before interrupting.

"That business has nothing to do with the weather. That man is a monster, and monsters like that are everywhere. Men rape young girls every day. Who knows about it? Who talks about it? This is the first time the press has spoken about such incidents."

"Yes, but he represents authority; he should provide an example and protect all citizens, male and female."

"Of course, it's an abuse of power. At his level it's visible, but on the level of a minor bureaucrat, you don't see it."

I should keep quiet. What's come over me to start preaching like this? I change the subject and ask Mr. Sabbane if everything is in order.

"Perfectly in order, Mr. Mourad. I just wanted to let you know that two documents were missing from the file. I have them in my briefcase and they require your signature."

He pulls them out as he's talking to me. I glance discreetly at Haj Hamid, who nods that we should finish up with this application. I scan the papers. It seems to me I've already seen them. I hesitate and sign.

Toward the end of the day, I am overcome with anxiety. I think of my children. I picture Karima's sad face again. I have to see her. I decide to take her on a trip to Tangier. A three-day vacation. I love the idea; the difficulties fall away. I'll tell Hlima that I have the right to go where I want with my daughter. I'll give Najia some time to think things over. I won't have to see the *chaouch* or Haj Hamid for seventy-two hours. I feel like a free man. This is only normal! I make decisions. I act. Is a corrupt man a free man? It's paradoxical: dirty money gives you wings. But what is that sort of freedom worth? I free myself from Hlima and her mother's domination. That's no small feat. But if I go all the way and remake my life with Najia, for instance, then I'll really have gained something. For the moment, the most important thing is to have a nice trip with my daughter. I'll surprise her. She'll skip school on Friday and we'll work on the train. I'll go by Najia's and talk to her. I'll dip into *Being and Nothingness* so we can travel in style.

HLIMA LOVES SCANDAL. SHE LOVES PASSING HERSELF OFF as a victim. Tonight, faced with my indifference, she'll shout, open the windows, call for the neighbors. Tonight will be my night. I'm preparing for it already. I take a sheet of paper and copy the following advice at least a hundred times: *Don't get excited. Stay calm.*

I arrive home, repeating this advice which is becoming unbearable to hear. Hlima is quiet. She's changed her strategy. She must be saving her strength for a more vicious attack later on. It's like certain animals who withdraw before attacking.

I change clothes. She follows me everywhere without speaking. I go into the children's room. Karima is sleeping on her French notebook. I stroke her hair. She slowly wakes up. She gives me a big smile and throws herself into my arms. I whisper in her ear to prepare her things, that we're leaving very early the next morning for Tangier.

THE TRAIN BETWEEN CASABLANCA AND TANGIER IS comfortable. Unfortunately it's also slow, almost six hours to travel 350 kilometers. I bring the book by Nietzsche with me. *Zarathustra* is a good companion. Reading it, listening to him, makes me feel better. Karima is an attentive girl; she's the one who always asks me if everything is all right, if I need anything. She also has brought a book: the fable of Kalila and Dimna, but she doesn't feel like reading. She's glued to the window, watching the landscape and commenting from time to time.

"There's an old woman walking in the fields, weighed down by a heavy bundle. There's a man following her on horseback. He's not nice. He should help her.

"The trees are moving fast.

"Those children are carrying jugs of water instead of going to school."

On the seat opposite us a middle-aged woman, a foreigner, has dozed off, a magazine open on her knees. The title of the

two-page spread reads: "Ten Tips for Having an Orgasm."
Maybe the lady is dreaming of one.

In Ksar el Kebir, a peasant gets on board and sits down next
to the foreigner. He smells of grass and hay. His face is hard.
When he looks at me I lower my eyes. Karima has fallen asleep.
I'm sleepy too, but the peasant is watching me. I close my eyes
and hear him stammering prayers. Maybe it's Mr. Sabbane in
disguise following me to ask for the envelope. He is grabbing
me by my shirt collar and threatening to strangle me. I wake
with a start. My saliva goes down the wrong way. I cough.
Karima wakes up. We've arrived in Asilah. The sea is beautiful,
sparkling. The brightness hurts your eyes. In the distance, we
see small white houses crammed one on top of the other. My
daughter says that the ocean is more beautiful here than in
Casablanca. "But it's the same one," I tell her. "No!" she replies,
"that's impossible." I don't argue with her.

SEEN FROM AFAR, TANGIER LOOKS LIKE A VOLUPTUOUS
princess, stretched out along the bay, her hair floating on the
sea. Upon arriving at the train station, we are jostled and surrounded by kids who propose something for everyone: a hotel,
a restaurant, a taxi, a house, American cigarettes, black-market
whiskey, Dutch cheese, hashish. Some offer nothing, but extend
their arms to help us carry our bags or to beg. Karima is tired
and hungry. We stop in front of a little kebab restaurant, take
a table opposite the beach, and eat with rare gusto.

I feel like we're in a foreign country, very far from home and
the office. It is rare for me to take a real vacation, to feel relaxed
and at rest. I do a quick calculation: two nights in the Minzah
Hotel plus the restaurant and cafés will cost me 1,500 DH. The
heck with saving money. I decide to give my daughter the best.
As soon as we get to the Minzah, Karima dives into the pool,
while I read *Zarathustra*.

In the afternoon, I telephone a childhood friend who has a travel agency. He used to work for a large company where, as he says, he "was keeping the theft machine from running smoothly." They called him "grain of sand" too, not because he's a small man but because he always placed himself in the administrative works to block corruption. One day, shortly after assuming his functions, the boss sent him to El-Huceima to buy a building for opening a branch of the company in the Rif. He had up to five hundred thousand dirhams at his disposal. Taking his role seriously, he found a site and haggled the price down to three hundred thousand dirhams. When he returned to Casablanca, he triumphantly announced to his boss that he had just saved the company two hundred thousand dirhams. Furious, the boss told him, "But no one asked you to bargain... You didn't understand. Your visit was only supposed to be a formality. You've spoiled everything." "On the contrary, I've settled everything," he responded. "The contract is signed and as far as I'm concerned the matter is closed!" After which, he got in the habit of nosing about everywhere until he found signs of theft and embezzlement. Since he was competent and irreproachable, the boss was unable to fire him. Instead he sent him abroad, to a country at war, with the unacknowledged goal of getting rid of him. There too he set about preventing corruption and was forced to return to Morocco the day his office and home were shelled.

The rest of his story was predictable. Eager for revenge, his manager fired him the day a coarse word slipped from him in conversation. "Grain of sand" found himself unemployed but proud of his integrity. He later started his own company.

WILL I DARE CONFESS TO HIM THAT I ENDED UP CAVING in, that I am no longer the same man and that a new life is beginning for me?

We get together and talk about the children and school expenses; about rising prices and being poor. He's surprised that I have taken a room at the most expensive hotel in town. I tell him I received a bonus and that these few days' vacation are a gift to my daughter. He doesn't seem convinced.

"You should have come to stay at our house," he tells me.

"Karima was dreaming of going to a hotel with a nice pool. It's a gift. It's not something I can give her every day."

He tells me about his lawsuit with the company that laid him off and reminds me that if he had stolen he never would have been fired.

We take a long walk around the city and dine together at his home. The next day, Karima accompanies Maria, my friend's daughter, to her riding club. When she gets back, she tells me all about it. "We'll see," I say.

On Sunday, at four in the afternoon, we get back on the train. Karima quickly falls asleep. I can't read. The party's over. I'm like a soldier returning from leave. I don't want to go back. I feel weak again, full of doubt. Voice B wells up inside me, without getting loud. It tells me what I already know: "Your friend deserves more credit than you. He's fighting sharks, corruption, an entire system. He's all alone. You lied to him. You've taken the first step in betraying your friendship. He works every day of the week to make ends meet, never takes a vacation, and thinks only of his children's future. It's true that his wife helps him a lot. She's content with what he brings home and doesn't demand more. She knows the situation and never pushed her husband to do like the others. You, on the other hand, resisted a long time, but you ended up caving under all the pressure. Now what will become of you? What are your plans? You'd like to start your life over with Najia, but do you have the means to satisfy the demands of such a beautiful young woman, so full of life and hope? Will you have the physical strength and energy necessary to win the war Hlima won't hesitate to wage? She'll fight this to the end because she's waited a long time and won't stand for someone else benefiting from what you call your 'bonuses.' She'll be formidable, intransigent, and fanatical; nothing will appease her. Perhaps this war will be over love; in any event, she'll never leave you in peace. My poor friend! You did well to give the little one these few days, even if it was with dirty money. She needed it. Now it's up to you to decide: either you go home, give back the money, and stay clean, or you make a break and see where it takes you. You forget that you're neither an adventurer nor a gambler. You're a simple, good-natured man stifled by integrity. Your entire life has been dominated by this scruple and now you're straying from what they call the straight path. Farewell, my friend! I leave you with the landscape and your thoughts."

IN KENITRA, A BEAUTIFUL YOUNG WOMAN BOARDS THE train with an older gentleman. She could be his daughter, but she is not, she's his wife. He, apparently, is rich, not a city dweller. She is probably a girl from a modest family. She's wearing too much makeup, too much jewelry, and is enveloped in strong perfume. She's rather clumsy. Her bag tips over as she sits down. On the seat are scattered bracelets and a gold chain, a thick billfold, a few crumpled hundred-dirham notes, two tubes of lipstick, a handkerchief, a hairbrush, a bunch of keys, and an amulet folded into a page of religious writing. When she bends over to gather up all these objects, I see her breasts clearly. She looks at me with a knowing smile. I help her put her things in order. The old man says to me:

"Women are the devil's nieces... they hide their faces behind powder and dust... and we, like little dogs, are at their feet, on our knees as you are right now."

I get up. "May God keep you from the devil and his children!" I say.

I look at her. Her eyes aren't cold. The old man has dozed off. I sense she's ready for anything. This type of woman scares me. Karima is slowly waking up. The woman takes advantage of the occasion to come sit next to us. She takes Karima in her arms, compliments her, and invites us to come to her house in Anfa. She gives me the address and phone number. Karima asks if she has children and a pool.

"No children, but a nice pool," she answers.

As we approach Casablanca, the husband wakes up and explains his presence on the train.

"My stupid driver just had his seventh child. No matter how much I tell him the planet is overburdened, he keeps getting his wife pregnant. That's why he couldn't pick us up in Kenitra. What a rude man! 'Just take the train,' he told me. What's this world coming to! No respect. Soon the rich will cease to exist!"

I DROP KARIMA OFF AT THE HOUSE, CHANGE MY CLOTHES, and get ready to go out. My wife stands in front of the door and bars me from leaving. She has the contents of a bottle of sleeping pills in her hand and threatens to swallow them all. I sit down and ask her to stop hamming it up. She screams her hatred and her pain. Meanwhile, on the television, there's an Egyptian soap opera in which an abandoned wife is shouting with all her might. I can't tell if I'm at home or in the soap opera. I turn off the television. My wife calms down, sits next to me, and asks forgiveness. I have never seen her in this state. She's ordinarily so strong and sure of herself; can she possibly be hanging her head and acting so meek? I suspect it's a trap, a strategy. "Stay firm, calm, don't give in," I tell myself. I see this home which no longer resembles me, this furniture, these sofa fabrics, these portraits on the wall. I contemplate the disorder and feel more and more like a stranger to it. My son comes in, his books under his arm. He says nothing, picks up a piece of fruit, and goes out again to study under the streetlamps.

Karima is sleeping. I try to talk to Hlima. I sense that the rift is deep and dates back farther than these last few days.

"If we've come to this breaking point today, you should know that your mother has a lot to do with it. Money worship turns everything it touches to rot. It has contempt for simple people, honest people incapable of being crooked. I carried this contempt around with me for a long time. I was even proud of it. The more your mother made me aware of it, the stronger my integrity became. But it's so hard to fight! I resisted as long as I could… Until one day I caved in, more to spare my children from poverty than to rid me of your mother's humiliation. You have always been on her side, so now go back to her, go live with her and leave me in peace. I'll fight so that my children want for nothing. I'll live without any luxuries until I secure their future. I'm leaving. Don't try to hold me back. There has been no love between us for a while now. Our life has become dull and depressing. We're not doing each other any good."

I walk out, leaving her dumbstruck by this settling of scores. I ring Najia's bell. No one is home. I try again. A neighbor opens the window and tells me she's gone on a trip. I find myself alone, tired, homeless. Should I go back home? Impossible. I decide to spend the night outdoors. I walk along Gandhi Boulevard. More and more high school and college students study on this well-lit street.

My son stops me.

"Where are you going, Dad?"

"Nowhere. I'm taking a walk. It's nice out." He offers to walk with me.

55

"Things aren't going well at home, Dad!"

"No, not very well. Life isn't easy. As soon as they have some money, people think they can push you around and step on your feet. How's school?"

"I work at it, but sometimes it's discouraging, especially when you realize you need connections to get anywhere. I want to go to one of the big schools. Sure, there are the competitive entrance exams, but a lot of times that's not enough, it takes a recommendation, and that's something you can't buy. And I'm like you, no corruption. In fact, if everyone were like us, the country would be in better shape. I like the Arabic word for corruption: it's what's consumed from the inside, eaten by moths, like wood that's rotted and good for nothing, not even for making a fire. It's the same thing with a man. If he sells his soul, if he buys off people's consciences, he participates in a process of general destruction. You know, bribery is like begging. Beggars exist because people give alms."

I listen to my son as we walk. I'm in pain and say nothing. He offers to take me back home and I accept. On the way, he tells me that two men came looking for me over the weekend. Maybe it was Haj Hamid, who thought I might like to join him on a round of the bars. I sit in the living room and read, but my thoughts are elsewhere. I put the book down and turn out the light. The night will be long and hard. My son's words run through my head. I'm ashamed. I decide to give the envelope back to Mr. Sabbane. At the moment, it's inside *Being and Nothingness*, which is on a bookshelf at Najia's. I hope she'll be home soon. Then I'll have to find someone to lend me money so I can repay what I've spent. It's something like two thousand dirhams. I bet Hlima will have it. I have to make up with her, but is now the time? Things are getting complicated. There's no proof I took the money. I could keep it and act like I don't have it.

Whoever said that night is a good adviser? They were wrong. Not only doesn't it advise, it overdramatizes the facts, blows them up, makes them weightier. I find myself in the tunnel where it's hard to move. Night is alarmist. I can't tear my feet off the ground. The soles of my shoes stick to the pavement when I try to walk. Each time I make an effort, my calves stretch. I'm sweating. I can't see the exit. Better to wake up and drink a glass of water. Nightmares die when you interrupt them. Unless they're so strong, so violent, that they wait for you to go back to sleep to resurface and wreak havoc in your head as it lies awkwardly on the pillow.

NOW I'M LUCID. I HAVE NO WAY OF TURNING BACK. MY guilty conscience can work all it wants. It's my conscience that throws me into the tunnel. If that's the price to be paid, so be it. I sign a contract with the tunnel pavement. I'll be there every night. I'll end up getting used to it. By dint of frequenting this land of shadows, I'll triumph over my demons. The heart, as the other voice says, must harden or break. No pity. No hesitation. It's time to make up for the empty years and dry seasons when nothing was going on.

The other voice kicks in: "Finally you're free, rid of scruples. You've put your finger, your hand, your entire arm in the works. It's time to forge ahead. You'll see, it's nothing. Now you have to change a certain number of elements in your behavior. I know, you've already noted what you should change, but it's not enough. You have to change the company you keep, go out, be seen, go to bars, pay for rounds of drinks, organize dinners, parties, you have to get into the slick mindset of a corrupt man. At first you'll feel uneasy, but after a few days you'll be so comfortable you'll get used to it and see the world with brand-new eyes. You don't get anything in life without taking risks. In any case, your shabby little life isn't worth much on the market. We could try to sell it at the lamb market on the eve of Aïd el Kebir, but I'm sure there'll be no crush to buy it. Who would want to get inside that dry little skin with room for only half a man? Who would rush to take on these forty-five miserable years? The risk is minimal to nonexistent. So, my friend, stop boring us with your scruples, which are making your family unhappy. Take advantage of Najia's naïveté, give her a little of your time and this money you say is dirty. Make her happy, if only for one week or one short season. Run, sing, shout, jump, get some color in your skin and put a little orange-flower water under your arms, change your hair, shave that ridiculous mustache, and don't look back—there is nothing to see. Move ahead and stop thinking!"

You're right, I have to stop thinking or I'll go mad. I know madness is out there, I feel it hovering around me, taunting me, promising to return and take hold of my reason.

Good. Let's be clear and efficient. Let's take one thing at a time: tomorrow morning on my way to the office, I'll stop by Najia's. If she's there I'll make a date for that evening. I have to talk to her. When I get to the office, I'll have coffee with the director. I know that's what Haj Hamid does. It's a sign between them. We'll talk about the rain and the fine weather. As we're leaving, I'll ask him if there are other applications. He's my boss but he's powerless without my signature. Thus, beginning tomorrow morning at eight o'clock, I will step inside the shoes of a corrupt bureaucrat. I'm not ashamed of the words. At noon I'll invite Haj Hamid to lunch. With him I think discretion and insinuation are unnecessary. I have to talk openly, put my cards on the table. I'll ask him advice about the house of my dreams. Maybe he can lend me some of the money. We'll see about that later. I must be content with one deal a week. A quick and approximate calculation tells me this could bring in between forty and fifty thousand dirhams a month, almost six months' salary. At that rate, if we factor in vacations, holidays, economic swings, the stinginess of certain contractors, and then a few luxuries—I'm capable of them, you'll see—I can bank on five hundred thousand a year. At that rate, only my death will stop this wonderful stream, a true treasure. The idea gives me wings, courage, and passion.

THIS MORNING I FEEL LIGHT. HLIMA IS MAKING ME COFFEE. I thank her. I even ask her if she needs anything. She says no. I go outside and hail a taxi. It's a Muslim brother: hanging prayer beads, open Koran, and a cassette of Abdessamad chanting the sura of the Cow. I don't dare light a cigarette. His eyes are dark. From time to time, he looks at me in the rearview mirror. His thick beard scares me. I too pray to God that these people will never come to power. "They are sons of corruption," my former philosophy professor, whom I run into from time to time at the French Cultural Center, told me one day. "Which means that the more corrupt ordinary people are, the more the Islamists will find a reason to exist and fight."

I'm anxious to get to the office. I have a busy day. I know that an application must be processed today. I rub my hands together. How is it I didn't fall into easy money sooner? Haj Hamid tells me that Mr. Sabbane is looking for me. "He must like me," I say, laughing.

In the afternoon, he comes into my office smiling, a fat folder under his arm. Haj Hamid excuses himself on the pretext of another meeting. It's strange. What's going on that I don't know about? Why am I suspicious?

Mr. Sabbane informs me that it's not his application. It belongs to an American company associated with a Moroccan group that wishes to invest in the construction industry. He's only an intermediary.

"I'm doing some friends a favor. Friendship is important. A good memory is important too."

He then explains the project to me, insists on the urgency of the matter and tells me he'll be back in two days. As soon as he leaves, I look for the envelope. There is none. How strange. Perhaps he'll pay when I sign. I don't want to talk to Haj Hamid about it. I study the documents. Everything seems in order. I decide to give a favorable opinion and pass it on to the director. He must know what it's about. I go upstairs to see him. As soon as I place the folder on his desk, he gets up and starts yelling about Mr. Sabbane, calling him a crook.

"This affair smells bad. Why is he acting as a middleman? I advise you to withdraw your approval. It must be a trap."

It must be that Mr. Sabbane snubbed him by coming directly to me. He won't get his commission, so he's moaning about it and would like to see the deal fall through. I take the folder and go back to my desk. I realize that illegality isn't so easy. It too has its rules, its written and unwritten laws, its signs and symbols. I'm ignorant. I'm just getting my feet wet in this swamp. What should I do? Refuse authorization? Delay examination of the application? What should I tell the intermediary, who must have other avenues open to him? What if he were to go directly to the minister? But the minister isn't going to handle such a small matter. He'll give it to the head of his cabinet, who won't hesitate to take the director of my office to task. In any case, the bonds are woven in such a way that everyone or almost everyone is implicated. As Mr. Sabbane says, a good memory is important. A good turn is a loan; one day or another it must be repaid.

The next day, Mr. Sabbane arrives early at my office. He says he's in a hurry and that he forgot to give me part of the file yesterday. He hands me a large yellow envelope and turns to go, wishing me a nice day. Inside is a small white envelope. I open it: a wad of new hundred-dollar bills. He's giving me dollars because of the American associates. I count quickly: four thousand dollars. Bills still smelling of printer's ink and with consecutive numbers. I hide the envelope and light a cigarette. Haj Hamid hasn't come back yet. I have the impression that things are getting complicated. It's either fear or a lack of habit. This money smells bad. I have to get rid of it. It has to be spent quickly. The telephone rings. I jump. As the doctor said, I'm overemotional, I'm weak. Everything affects and upsets me. It's Najia calling. I'm surprised and don't know what to say to her. She tells me to come to her house that evening, after her daughter has eaten supper. I'm both happy about this and worried. I don't like making decisions. I get scared when I'm forced into it. I like to delay the moment of choice as long as possible. Najia is certainly going to ask me to decide. I am beginning to miss the days when everything was calm and tranquil. I was living miserably but without any major problems. Now everything takes on dramatic proportions. Everything is serious, a telephone call, an appointment, a signature, a drive by the ocean, a look from Haj Hamid, a gesture from the *chaouch*, the color of the sky, the taste of the coffee, the exchange rate of the dollar, the cost of living—everything takes on disturbing proportions.

Najia's voice is clear, that of a women who knows what she wants. Hlima knows what she wants too. It's the means employed that differ. Hlima is surly, vindictive, and greedy. She's pushed by her mother. And they say that Moroccan women are oppressed, dominated, and abused! Some of them, yes, but not my mother-in-law, and not her daughters or nieces or cousins. Why does she pick on me though? Poverty is a defect, it's like being born one-eyed or hunchbacked. And if it's a defect of nature, should nature be blamed? Even if I become rich, she'll continue to attack me, because in her eyes I'll still be a former pauper.

I LEAVE THE OFFICE EARLIER THAN USUAL. I LOOK AT THE sky and wonder why I have such a reflex. What sense does it make to lift one's head and fill one's eyes with blue? None. It's a question of habit. From now on I mustn't waste time. I must be fast and efficient, clear and resolute. In either case, whether with Hlima or Najia, I need to be firm in my determination. If only I knew what I should be determined about! Let's see what happens, wait and see. Don't get excited. No hasty decisions. Think, analyze, reflect calmly, without hurrying, weigh every-thing. Whatever you do, don't hurry. I am going to see Najia now. She has known for several years that one day or another our paths would cross; that's why she found it entirely natural for me to ring her bell and confide in her. Our relationship must have started long ago, silently, below the surface. The time to take stock of it is here. How scary! I feel confused, weak. What can I offer such a beautiful widow? And why should she have chosen me? It's true I helped her a little. Now I have to face reality. What a test!

NAJIA IS WAITING FOR ME. I GO HOME FIRST, KISS KARIMA, eat a piece of fruit and leave. Hlima says nothing. Her face is tired. She is watching her home go down the drain, powerless to do anything.

Najia has just put her daughter to sleep. She hugs me and kisses me. I feel her feverish body in my arms. I want her. Her hands push me away. I understand that this is not the right moment. She begins talking.

"I went away for a few days to my aunt's house in Fez and thought things over. I think I love you and would be happy if we could marry. My mother admitted to me that the nursing story was a joke."

I remain silent. That was it. Not surprising. She takes my hand and kisses it. I glance around for *Being and Nothingness*.

It's still in its place. I hand her my briefcase and ask her to take an envelope from it.

"It's American money! You're rich!"

"We're rich!"

"Where does it come from?"

"From a commission."

"What commission?"

"The commission that every self-respecting bureaucrat receives when he successfully concludes a deal…"

"But that's corruption!"

"Not exactly. Corruption is when you make someone pay for something that's his by right. For example, every citizen has the right to a passport. If, in addition to the revenue stamp, the administrator demands a sum of money that is not recorded, that's called corruption."

"But that's a minute distinction. This money is dirty. I didn't know you were like this, capable of stealing from society, from the state, from the people."

"Let's not exaggerate. I didn't steal from anyone, and especially not from the people. This money was given to me by an American company. After all, this sort of thing goes on even in developed countries. The rest of us are amateurs."

"I'm sorry. You're disappointing me. What attracted me to you was your integrity, your dignity. Honest men are so rare. That's why I wanted to live with you. I'm sorry… I made a mistake."

She starts crying. I'm ashamed. I should have lied. It's not always a good idea to tell the truth. It wasn't very smart of me. I try to calm her down. The harm has already been done. It's too late. I've lost. I've lost everything. I'm desperate but I'm not going to start crying. Nothing can be done. I put the envelope in my briefcase, take *Being and Nothingness*, and head for the door. Will she hold me back? She's a strong, good woman; she's not going to give in. She lets me go. I find myself out on the street at ten o'clock at night. Crushed, cruelly demolished, I can hardly move. If only I could tolerate alcohol, I would get drunk and forget this difficult moment. I walk along, thinking of my unhappiness and solitude. I think of my daughter and our escapade in Tangier. I'm ashamed. I'm not worthy. I've ruined everything, destroyed everything, and I don't understand what is happening to me. Najia's the one I should have made my life with. She would never have pushed me toward corruption. I'm a victim of my weakness and my illusions.

I don't feel up to going home right away. I'll wait until very late at night. If Hlima sees me in this defeated state, she'll take advantage of it.

As I'm walking I bump into a woman in a black djellaba. I apologize and she stops. What is a young woman doing on the street at this hour? I turn around. "You look beat up," she says, approaching me. "Come, I'll make you a glass of tea."

I follow her without arguing. If she has pity on me, so much the better. What do I care if she's a prostitute or a thief? She can have the dollars. Then I pull myself together. No, this money belongs to me. It took me over twenty years to earn it.

We walk in silence with hurried steps. When we arrive at a dilapidated building, she tells me:

"Pay no attention, these people are dirty. They throw garbage in the entrance to the building. They're country people who don't know how to live in the city. Some of them even urinate on the wall. There's no light in the stairwell, because every time the bulb is replaced, someone steals it. Be careful with your briefcase; sometimes there are kids lurking in the dark who grab people's bags."

I climb the stairs without commenting. It smells bad. Behind the doors you can hear the shouts of Egyptian actors on television. The Egyptian films of our childhood were marvelous, but the programs they show on television nowadays are terrible. That's what decadence is all about. The actors shout instead of acting. They participate in the collective hysteria. And more and more, Moroccans are acting and speaking like their Egyptian idols. It's reached epidemic proportions. If I had the power, I would create a new form of censorship: ban mediocrity! If I had the power, I wouldn't even have to notice that these programs existed, or I'd be happy to keep people occupied with such nonsense.

I arrive on the fifth floor breathless and begin to wonder what on earth I'm doing here. She opens the door. A cat runs out and rubs against her legs. Who is she? Who sent her? I stop asking myself questions and look around. Two clean, tidy rooms. On the wall is a photo of the Egyptian singer Mohamed Abdelwahab. That's a sign of quality. Next to it, a photo of her, arm in arm with an elegant old man.

"That's my father. He died a few days after this picture was taken."

I follow her into the kitchen where she prepares some tea. A clock-radio is sitting on the table. It's 11:10 PM. I look at my watch and find it's three minutes slow.

When she takes off her djellaba, I notice just how young she is.

"You must be wondering why I invited you to my house," she says. "It was a crazy, irrational gesture. I've never done this before. I'm a student, an orphan. I live alone and work nights as a nurse in the hospital. I'm studying medicine and I also like to write; I do lots of things, as you can tell. I'm curious. I was afraid to come home alone, so I got the better of my fear: when I saw you, I knew immediately you were as alone as I was and that you wouldn't hurt me."

"You're very nice, but reckless."

"I know. I spend all day at school, and three nights a week at the hospital, so sometimes I need a change of pace. After we drink our tea, I'll send you home."

"You're wonderful."

"Oh, I'm just who I am, I don't try to be anything I'm not."

"Thanks for bumping into me."

"It was chance. Why are you so sad?"

"I was a peaceful man, married with two children. I had a good job, and then I teetered, I lost my balance. I made a mistake, I sinned, and now I think I'm spreading unhappiness around me. It would take too long to explain, and I don't want to bore you."

She stands up. Now her face is well lit. There's something strange about it. It seems as if one eye is dead. The left one, to be specific. I verify this in a flash. It doesn't respond, it doesn't follow me. I'm a little uncomfortable and I think she recognizes my discomfort.

"Yes, I see out of only one eye. I lost the other one when I was little. That's why I bumped into you. Well, I'm going to sleep. I'll leave you a phone number where you can reach me at night at the hospital. If you want to talk or drink a glass of tea, call me. My name is Nadia."

I thank her and leave, almost breaking my neck on the stairs. I think of how open she is and marvel at how surprising Moroccan woman are. I believe everything she has told me. Is she a pathological liar? Perhaps. An adventuress? No doubt. It's after midnight. I return home. Tomorrow, God, the sky, Najia, or Nadia will help me find peace again.

WHILE SHAVING IN THE MORNING I NOTICE THREE NEW wrinkles beneath each eye and a small white spot behind my ear. Before, my face never changed. It was always the same with just a natural fatigue or sadness. Now I sense I've crossed over the line. But Haj Hamid's face exudes well-being. I'll never be a corrupt man without wrinkles. I think too much, I'm such a bad operator. Earlier, Hlima asked where I spent the night. Instead of calmly telling her the truth, I made up stories and raised my voice. Do I look like someone who keeps a mistress? No! I look like a poor guy who doesn't know how to get out of the way of a machine that's going to crush him. I can see the machine from here, approaching at a regular pace. It's getting nearer. Sometimes it's led by Haj Hamid, sometimes by Mr. Sabbane, sometimes by Nadia, whose facial features are blurred. In the meantime, what do I do? I moan and groan. I beg the mirror to send me a different image, that of the honest man I have been all my life. But nothing can be done. It can't be fixed.

I don't know what day it is anymore, but what difference does it make? I'm going to get rid of the dollars. If I convert them, I'll feel like I've done a little something to earn them. It's symbolic, an illusion. By transforming them into dirhams, I'll at least feel I've contributed to bringing hard currency into the state treasury. But will that be enough to erase their dubious origin?

I CHOOSE A BANK I'VE NEVER GONE TO BEFORE. AT MY bank the teller knows me and would suspect something. The hall is large and cold. The architecture dates from the French period. It's solidly built, which is normal; a bank has to be solid. I'm afraid of my timidity. It could give me away or cause me to make a false move. The man behind the window has a fat face, obstructed by a mustache. All his gestures are quasi-mechanical. He counts the bills with lightning speed. Without even looking at me, he slides a form under the glass to be filled out. I step aside and read it carefully. It's written in French. I could act smart and demand a form in Arabic or at least a bilingual one. But I won't act smart. Among the information requested is my national identity card number. I write it down. The man behind the window looks up at me for the first time, stares for a few seconds, and asks for my card. I slide it under the glass and wait. He gets up, goes to the back, and returns. I decide to change only half the money. All of a sudden, I think of my son, who wants to learn English in the United States. I could pay for his trip. I'll tell him the money was lent to me by a childhood friend who lives in America. The teller counts the dollars with a steady speed, except that he is forced to wet his index finger often because the bills are so new.

"This money has never been used!" he points out to me.

"Perhaps," I respond.

I feel like ordering him to stop looking at me suspiciously, stop commenting and hurry up and give me the equivalent in dirhams. But I don't move. I wait. Before giving me a ticket for the cashier's window, he verifies my address and asks if I have a telephone number at my office. I give it to him. He writes it down, making me repeat it twice. This is overdoing it!

The cashier doesn't look at me. He reads the amount, opens a drawer, and removes bundles of one- and two-hundred-dirham notes. I don't count them. Actually, I try to count along with him but I can't. I put them in my briefcase and exit whistling.

Wow! What an ordeal! Where am I going to stash the money? Shouldn't I give it back to Mr. Sabbane? No, I'm not in the mood to go backwards anymore.

Nothing is new at the office. The routine, or almost. Just a telephone call from the bank to verify that the number is correct.

I feel like calling Nadia but I have to wait until evening. As for Najia, I don't know if she'll let me see her again. I'll try at the end of the day. I decide to calm the situation at home. I'll give half the money to Hlima so she can buy the gold belt she's been dreaming of. All her sisters have one. Whenever she has to go to a wedding with the rest of her family, she cries. As far as she's concerned, a married woman must have a gold belt. I don't know if this will be enough, but I'll tell her it's an advance. I'll have a little peace. I'll even be able to go out at night, to see Najia or Nadia. She won't suspect a thing. She won't ask me any questions about the source of the money. She knows that most bureaucrats practice flexibility! I've become a flexible man. I am sorry for the trouble of these last weeks. Life is smiling on me. Haj Hamid is too. Except that I don't like his smiles. He's a hypocrite. He'll go to hell. As my mother says, "He's crooked in his gut." In his gut, his head, his hands, his feet, his walk, his talk, his eyes... everything.

I think again of the dead eye on such a beautiful face. It's unfair. I'm sure such a thing will never happen to H.H. From now on I'll call him H.H. He'll think he's famous, like a character on an American television show. In Arabic, with the aspirated *h*, it sounds like *ha-ha*, ridiculous. H.H. has a double life. I know this and I think even his wife knows it. He showers her with gifts and money and she buys herself jewelry; he's the one who told me so one day. She has two gold belts. He considers them an investment, even if the price of gold doesn't fluctuate much. He shares a bachelor flat with a friend who's as corrupt as he is, a certain Taïbi, who specializes in the purchasing of equipment at a ministry. He gets his girls at the entrance to the high school and sometimes on the university campus. Life smiles on them. The girls fall like flies. From time to time he organizes an orgy. H.H. invited me the other day. "It's time you were part of the club, now that you're rich. .." he told me. I didn't answer. How can he be so lacking in scruples? Why can't I be happy? I ask myself so many questions. I know that everything has its price: a moment of deviation, an instant of happiness, of forgetfulness... everything. I pay, whereas life gives H.H. and his cohorts credit on long, very long terms. They're never bothered, never in a hurry to settle up.

AT NIGHT, I RING NAJIA'S BELL. HER MOTHER OPENS THE door, invites me in and offers me a glass of tea. Najia has just gone to the grocery store. Her mother asks me for news of Hlima and the children. She goes to the kitchen and leaves me alone in the living room. "You'll eat with us," she says when she comes back. "It's simple, but it'll be good." I don't know what to say. Najia might not want me to stay for dinner. I mumble something polite and close my eyes. When I open them, Najia is standing before me. Cordial and even welcoming. She speaks to me in French:

"Excuse me for yesterday, I was too harsh. After all, it's your life, you should do as you like. Don't involve me in your trafficking. You'll always be welcome here, but I refuse to having anything to do with dirty money. It's a principle of mine. In this country there are still some people who respect principles. They're rare but they exist and one mustn't sully them. Besides, it's partly thanks to them that the country functions. Not all Moroccans are corrupt."

Of course, even if corruption is like a plague, a "parallel and underground economy," as a former militant socialist put it, it hasn't affected all Moroccans.

It is neither the time nor the place to carp about this disease, which is widespread and apparently beneficial to a segment of those who contract it.

Najia is angry. If I were really corrupt, someone who could have naturally integrated this practice into his life, no one would have noticed the sudden change in me. I discover, or rather I confirm, that I'm not cut out for this business.

I admit this to Najia, who doesn't listen to me. I feel as if I'm talking to myself and that whatever I do, I'll never be able to regain her trust and respect.

I could call Nadia. Maybe things would be easier with her. But I have no feelings for her. Just a bit of physical attraction. I recall the generous curves of her body. I think of her now and feel my desire building. I no longer know whether I desire Najia, who is standing before me as I think of Nadia, or whether it's an abstract desire without an object, as when I'm alone and touch myself.

Najia puts the books and a few belongings in a plastic bag and bids me farewell.

I leave, my anger held in check, ready to let off steam with Nadia's body. She is waiting for me in a robe. Without saying a word we put our arms around each other and head toward the bed. I close my eyes. Her entire body is feverish. We undress while kissing. We're naked. I avoid encountering her dead eye. I mustn't think about it. Just as I am about to penetrate her, she pushes me away gently, gets up, and brings me a condom. I lose my erection. I try putting it on but I can't. I'm not used to making love with a condom. She puts on a bathrobe, smokes a cigarette, then lies down next to me. She strokes me in repeated and various ways until my penis rises; with her soft, firm fingers, she slips the condom on.

IN THE MORNING, I STOP AT HOME TO CHANGE. HLIMA IS crying. She tells me that two men came by last night. She's sure they're with the police.

"What have you done now, you wretch? Not only do you abandon your wife and children and hang out with prostitutes, but in addition you get nabbed like a child! You must have been set up. This takes the cake. The first time you dare to be a man, a real man, your innate clumsiness does you in. If you go to prison, don't count on me to bring you bread and olives. Ask the whores you've been moaning over. Here, they left this letter. It must be a summons. It's incredible, in this country everyone dabbles in corruption and no one gets caught. But it suffices for Mr. Mourad, Mr. Virtue, Mr. Morality, to receive a tiny little commission for the police to dash to his home. You can see it on your face that you took some money that wasn't very clean. It's written on your forehead. What a shame! What luck!"

I let her talk. The two men couldn't be police. Their letter isn't official. No Ministry of the Interior letterhead. It's a white paper with the words *We'll be back!* on it. Let them come back. I have nothing to be afraid of. H.H. has stolen millions. He's never been worried. Our boss just bought a building for two million. He couldn't have made such an acquisition on his salary. Really, if they decide to fight corruption, they've got to start with the big fish, the ones who are visibly getting rich. Everyone knows it and nothing happens to them. Nothing scares them. Nothing. They're left alone, never worried. They're not going to punish me for a few thousand dirhams, are they? No, the two men must be friends of H.H.'s. It must be a delicate matter. It's not wise to talk at the office, so they preferred to come see me at home. They're right, I can understand that.

I ARRIVE AT THE OFFICE IN A TAXI. THE *CHAOUCH* IS polite but looks at me pityingly, as if I were on death row. H.H. gives me a less cordial welcome; he comes to me gloomily, as if to announce bad news.

"Two men came by yesterday in the late afternoon. I didn't know them and they didn't say who they were. They'll be back this morning. I hope it's a mistake. In any case, you can count on me if there's trouble. Be careful, though, don't name names

72

whatever you do. If they nab you, I can talk to the right person who knows a judge who knows what to do… If need be, a few thousand dirhams will take care of it. Besides, I checked it out. Corruption of a state worker will get you around three years of prison. And first they have to prove a bribe was taken. There are two possibilities: one, you confess, or two, they set a trap and catch you red-handed. The second hypothesis is out, which leaves the first. You have to deny everything. Anyway, your lifestyle is not, to my knowledge, that of a rich man, so you have nothing to be afraid of. You don't even own a car… You can relax. I'm your partner and a true friend—I hope you think of me as a friend—and I can testify to your exceptional integrity, your moral sense, your good work, and, quite simply, to your honesty."

"Thanks for your support," I reply. "As for friendship, that's a rare and precious thing. I only have one friend and he's in Tangier. But if he learns that I'm suspected of what they call 'flexibility,' he'll withdraw his friendship. He's pure. For him, it would be like a betrayal of our bond. Since you're sure I'm neither being suspected nor accused, I can relax, or at least I can try."

H.H. is buried in his newspaper. He avidly follows the affair of the police commissioner in charge of political security who raped over five hundred women. He raves on and on and can't contain his anger.

"Condemned to death… That's all? But he has to pay, he has to suffer. They have to drive him mad. Death is just an endless sleep. He deserves worse."

THAT NIGHT, I HAVE THE SAME DREAM FOR THE hundredth time: I'm on a terrace fairly high up. Everyone else uses the outside ladder to get down. My father, my brother, the neighbor. I'm frozen with fear. When I approach the

ladder, I'm convinced an invisible hand is going pull it away.
So I wait. The dream is steeped in darkness. Fortunately the
desire to urinate wakes me, or I'd stay in this state until
morning.

Not only does H.H. sleep well, but he probably never has
nightmares. He is talking about a weekend in Agadir with
his buddies; they're going there to play cards and spend the
night with beautiful girls. He shows me pictures of his last
trip, which he hides in the office. His wife never comes to get
him and she doesn't call either. From time to time, his eldest
daughter comes to see him. A beautiful piece of sculpture. He's
worried about her. He goes to the window when she leaves to
make sure she's not with a man. He wants to marry her off. I
tease him. "She's still young," I tell him, "she hasn't finished
school." Like many fathers in his position, he gets straight to
the point: "I'm responsible for her virtue. Such a beautiful girl
is a load of problems, of worries and anxiety. In this country
men have no shame about taking advantage of young girls'
innocence and naïveté. Just go to the high school when it lets
out. There are more Mercedes than students. And the girls get
in! That's the tragedy. They get in with men who could be their
fathers... That I cannot accept. I know my daughter is very
serious. But I don't know her girlfriends. That's my big worry!"

He's all worked up. But, curiously, he doesn't see himself as
someone "who has no shame about taking advantage" of
young girls' innocence and naïveté!

I calm him down by reiterating that his daughter is quite
serious. The truth is, I don't believe any of what I'm saying.
The way she looked at me when her father turned his back
says a lot about her supposed naïveté. She must be playing him
for a fool. I'm sure she has more than one lover and that she
just plays at being daddy's little girl. She'll end up marrying
some good-looking rich boy. It's like a romance novel. In fact,

I noticed a book called *The Two of Us* sticking out of her bag. She seems like a flighty young girl who cares only about luxury and comfort. H.H. is right to worry. I confess that it brings me a certain pleasure. To each his worries. For the time being, mine keep piling up. For one thing, I don't know what the two men looking for me want. If they were from the police, they'd have left a summons. A blue paper. I got one once, a long time ago, when the owner of our apartment wanted to evict us. I paid my rent regularly, but he was claiming I didn't. I paid him in cash and he never gave me a receipt. It's a story that taught me how malicious people can be. I trusted him and he was scheming behind my back. He had bribed a judge so that his case would get moved ahead of the others. The judge sent the order to the police, who summoned me. Fortunately, I gathered a dozen or so witnesses and the case was dismissed. Since then, I pay by check and he gives me a receipt.

So it isn't the police. Unless it's that special anticorruption squad the public prosecutor set up but which never actually assumed its duties. With my luck, if this squad ever starts up in earnest, I'm sure they'll begin with me.

I think of Karima, of her future. For the time being, she doesn't give me anything to worry about. I'm the one who worries her. What with my disappearances, my outbursts, and especially my nervousness, she must be concerned, though she says nothing. Tonight I'll go straight home and spend time with her, I swear.

THE DIRECTOR CALLS US IN FOR A MEETING. H.H. ADJUSTS his tie, combs his hair, and grabs his briefcase.

"After you, boss!"

I walk ahead; he approaches and whispers in my ear:

"I suspect the director of hanging around my daughter. I saw his Mercedes one day at the entrance to her school. He's a skirt-chaser whose motto is 'Under twenty.'"

When we arrive, H.H. greets the director respectfully. We're the first ones there; he asks us about our children and H.H. looks at me knowingly. The director asks me how old my daughter is.

"Thirteen, sir."

"May God bless her and keep her from evil... We live in a time of weak morality. Better to have only boys. I wouldn't want to be the father of daughters between sixteen and twenty. All my daughters are married. Now I'm a grandfather. I don't have to worry about their virtue anymore. It's their husbands' problem."

A NORMAL MEETING. NOTHING SPECIAL. THE ROUTINE. THE director reviews the projects submitted to us, examines the bids, then as usual gives us his little ethics lecture. In the mean-time, I drift off. I listen with one ear to what he's saying and immerse myself in a wonderful daydream. This time, I stay close by. I join my daughter at her school, sit with her in her seat and watch her. She is lively, intelligent, attentive, curious about everything. She seems to be more well-adjusted in class than at home. I tell myself that all parents should go watch their children without being seen. Perhaps my imagination is trying to boost my spirits. And why not? If only I could sit on a branch, like a sparrow, and watch Najia in her school or in the privacy of her home! I don't even know whether what I feel for her is love or simple physical attraction at a difficult moment in my life. I can't see myself living with her as husband and wife. Oddly enough, I was never prepared for this type of life. My marriage was more for convention's sake than for love. I loved Hlima, but as soon as I met her mother I knew that she was going to meddle in our lives and destroy our love. Between her husband and her tribe, Hlima has always chosen her mother's clan. Little by little, the feelings of love have dwindled. Between us only a small hatred cloaked in habit and sadness has survived. Now all I care about is my children's future. My life is almost over. I don't have the strength to fight anymore. Maybe I should have confronted Najia. I capitulated right away, I didn't defend myself. I must say that I'm not very sure of my recent actions, nor very proud. I gave in to pressure and don't know how to act, how to behave. I think again of the two men who are looking for me. I couldn't stand for them to touch me. Yet I know that once you walk through the door of the police station, you no longer have any rights. There are laws, certainly, but they remain theoretical. The mentality of the police hasn't changed. First, they manhandle you, then you talk. It's common practice. I'm talking about ordinary incidents, not political ones. The various human-rights organizations have succeeded in reducing the "close watch" to forty-eight hours, but when will they change police mentalities?

I suddenly ask myself the question: Is corruption an infraction of ordinary criminal law or a political offense? Is accepting a bribe to favor one application over another political? That depends on the nature of the application.

I'm starting to be afraid. I feel my stomach knotting and my blood flowing at one moment too quickly, then too slowly. There are beads of sweat on my forehead. I wipe my brow. The director watches me and asks if I'm feeling all right. I assure him I'm okay. It's warm. It's always warm when you're afraid. I've never been very brave. It's because of my father, who told us, "The fearful shall be saved!" and quoted these words of the Prophet: "The best is at the center." He didn't like extremes. He knew that life doesn't give you any gifts. So he didn't make a fuss. The truth is, he was honest out of a lack of audacity and courage. I resemble him: until now I didn't accept bribes partly out of fear of being caught. Then you work it out with your conscience, you conclude that you really do have integrity and that you're promoting principles and laws and standards.

Once we're back in our office, the *chaouch* brings us some tea. My first swallow goes down the wrong pipe, and I almost choke. It's a sign of nervousness. I don't feel well. I envy all those who can lie, cheat, and steal in good health. H.H. advises me to take a sick day. But I'm not going to visit a doctor because I'm sick from fear and a bad conscience, am I? Unless I go to a psychiatrist, who would know how to listen to me and even treat me. I gather my belongings and decide to go see a doctor after all, a friend of H.H.'s. They play cards together and he probably knows this fear syndrome, the "syndrome of the corruption novice." I suppose you have to go through this before you stop hurting yourself, holding yourself in contempt and imagining catastrophes.

THE DOCTOR TELLS ME I AM OVEREMOTIONAL AND TIMID. He gives me a sedative. I sleep better, but in the morning I feel tired. As for timidity, it's been working against me for some time now, to the point of making me even smaller than I am. It crushes me and pushes me down. I feel persecuted by this curse. At school, I used to blush whenever the teacher looked at me. Until the age of twenty, I avoided shaking people's hands because mine were so damp. When my first child was born, I gained a little self-confidence and conquered a small part of this illness. In times of crisis, it gets twice as bad.

How should I dress if I'm summoned by the police? I have two suits and five shirts. If I put on the navy-blue suit, the poor cops will think I'm trying to taunt them. If I'm sloppy, it'll look as if I intentionally dressed to pass for a minor bureaucrat content with his miserable salary.

Appearances are important. Here in Morocco, books are judged by their covers. Well, maybe not always. But here, people don't like naturalness or simplicity. You have to go to the country to meet people who are still attached to the simple things in life. They're welcoming and generous, even though they're poor. In the city, the richer the people the more calculating they are. My mother-in-law has a calculator behind her eyes.

IT'S STRANGE, THE WHITE SPOT BY MY EAR HAS GROWN. I touch it but I don't feel anything. I look at the other ear. A white dot has appeared. It's my liver. I read in a women's magazine that this kind of spot indicates that your liver is tired. Why should mine be tired? I drink almost no alcohol, I don't like chocolate, and I'm very careful about what I eat. But that doesn't mean anything. People who are careful attract problems; those who are carefree are often in good health. Nothing happens to them. Problems avoid them; they don't find enough uneasiness in which to develop.

I'd better consult a specialist. Even for that I need a referral. Just thinking about it, I feel a pain in my right side where my liver is. No, I'm not sick. It's anxiety, it gives you blemishes. I have more and more white spots on my skin; dirty money is provoking these cutaneous eruptions. I'm going to become an albino. The police won't even need to question me; all they'll have to do is undress me to see that my blood is allergic to corruption. It's not very logical. If it worked that way there'd be so many albinos the country would have to change its name, even its territory! I'm looking at people on the street, searching for a victim like myself. I feel like asking H.H. to take his shirt off. You'd think his whole body would be covered in these kinds of spots. Maybe he puts makeup on them. Does he wear a mask? Does he powder his face? I don't dare get close enough to examine him. I talk to him about this problem. Without looking up from the sports page he tells me that it's common at first, and that then the body adjusts. "We all go through this. It's normal. It's a change of life. We go from one state to another. Of course, there's a disturbance. The blood no longer circulates at the same rate. Don't get panicked. You'll see, it'll go away as you get used to it. Avoid drinking champagne and eating lobster!" No doubt about it, he takes me for a fool. I don't mind going without lobster for the simple reason that I've never eaten any. How could I miss it? I don't even drink. A little glass of French wine from time to time, or some whiskey on the rocks. I was afraid he'd forbid me from smoking. It's my only luxury: filling my lungs with nicotine and tar. It's my consciously destructive and fatalistic side. Nonetheless, I should stop poisoning myself, at Karima's ever so sweet and tender request, which she whispered in my ear: "This is a secret between us. If you love me, stop smoking. It hurts me when I hear you coughing in the morning. You don't want your daughter to be in pain, do you?"

Hlima's silences and apparent indifference worry me. I thought that in time our love would turn to friendship. Alas, it has slowly died out, unraveled, and given way to resentment. Because of the children, I have accepted many things. But it no longer makes sense to stay together.

IT HURTS MY DAUGHTER WHEN I COUGH. HOW WILL SHE feel if tomorrow I'm thrown in prison? And why would I go to prison? What have I done that's worse than the others? I've barely started to break the law and already I see myself confined to four damp walls. I imagine too much. I should have worked in film; I would have made a good screenwriter. For the moment, my life is the only victim of my overflowing imagination. I have always gotten ahead of events. Not that I'm clairvoyant but, as my father used to say, I see the consequences of things before they even happen. It's called worrying.

So how could I not have foreseen that my gums would

recede? They've been bleeding for a long time. I should have been more farsighted. My vision is still good. If tomorrow I suffer a detachment of the retina, it will be an accident. What can I predict from these white spots? They're probably psychological, they couldn't be physical. I'm not sick. Although... I don't feel very well. I have to stop thinking. It's the only way. I've become allergic to paper. Maybe it's the paper that's provoking the white spots.

H.H. arrives at the office, furious.

A team of inspectors has announced its visit for this afternoon. He's worried because he doesn't know any of them. You never know. Even if they can be bought, there are forms to respect. There's a limit to what you can say. What might he be afraid of? Bribes leave no trace. An envelope changes hands. That's all. No witnesses. No writing. Nothing. It's the perfect transaction. That's why they talk about liquidity. Money circulates, it flows; bills pass from one pocket to another and they haven't invented a machine yet to detect their origin. Can you imagine running a hundred-dirham bill past the laser of a machine that would generate the names of everyone who'd touched it?... But what would that prove? In principle, the machine should do more than that, but in any case it hasn't been invented yet. Even if it existed, the Mafia would break it.

H.H. is worried and I'm not. Usually it's the reverse. Let's just say that everything is in order with me and I have nothing to feel guilty about. Except perhaps they'll ask me for the old typewriter that no one was using anymore. When they replaced it with an electric, I borrowed it for a few days at home. My son typed an assignment on it. Since then, I admit I've kept it at home. Karima uses it from time to time; she taught herself to type. If they look for it, I'll bring it back. I'll say I just borrowed it for a few days. That's all that's missing. The files are in order. The office is clean. Our secretary is still out on sick leave.

There's nothing to worry about. But H.H. has gotten into the habit of "cutting deals" before anything is even asked of him. A lot of people are like that. They begin by looking for the person to whom the envelope, whether fat or thin, should be slipped, even when they're strictly within their most basic rights. How can you fight such a scourge, and how can you resist it?

THE *CHAOUCH* COMES IN FIRST, ANNOUNCING, "THE gentlemen of the Commission." There are three of them. They all have mustaches, probably in honor of their hero, Saddam. Even before hearing them, I suspect that they support him. If we had time, I would gladly tell them about that little village, Halabjah, that was gassed by Saddam's army. But this is neither the time nor the place to talk politics. And I mustn't give them an opportunity to look for trouble with me either. Their chief is a fat little man, dressed in a gray suit, blue sweater, beige shirt, and a blue and red striped tie. He's bald, but his few remaining hairs are plastered to his head, as if he's glued them on. The other two are just ordinary. Nothing in particular to note. The tallest one, who is the worst dressed, bites his nails. At a certain point, I catch him putting his finger in his nose. He pulls it out fast and looks away. People who pick their noses or clean their ears don't like to be caught in the act. It's only normal; they know it's disgusting. I didn't mean to look. I hope he won't try to take revenge. People who have dirty little habits aren't always clean, morally or physically. I see he's blowing his nose now. It's as if he's doing it to justify the other gesture. I couldn't care less. But he must think I'm as snotty-nosed as he is. He approaches the secretary's desk and remarks that there's a lot of carbon paper.

"We're economizing," I tell him. "We don't buy ribbons anymore. They're too expensive. The machine prints directly on the carbon paper and then we save money on photocopies too!"

"That's a pretty petty savings," he answers.

They sit down around H.H.'s desk. Each one picks up a stack of files and begins skimming through them. From time to time, one of them stops, mumbles something in the boss's ear, and continues. H.H. and I look at each other. He is more worried than I am. All of a sudden, the boss gets up and starts scanning the room for something. H.H. asks if he can help. He shakes his head no and comes toward me.

"There is some equipment missing. I see on the list: a wooden coatrack, an electric calculator, an Olivetti manual typewriter... All of these have disappeared."

I explain to him that the typewriter was replaced.

"And the old one? Did you sell it?"

"No, sir. The old one is rusted, I brought it home to fix. I'm good at fixing things. The coatrack we put in the hall. It was taking up too much room here."

"And the calculator?"

"It's there, in the right-hand drawer of Haj Hamid's desk. We don't use it much. I bought a small Japanese battery-powered calculator with my own money. That's what I use."

H.H. smiles. It seems they have discovered nothing. At lunchtime they look at one another and ask us to recommend a good restaurant. H.H. tells them that a restaurant is out of the question and invites us to eat at his house. I would never have dared bring them to my house. It's a minor form of corruption. They accept without his having to insist, as if they were expecting it.

We get into H.H.'s Mercedes. The boss asks me what kind of car I have. I think a second. Is this a trick question? If I lie and tell him, say, a Renault 25, he might consider that I do well for a public official. If I tell him the truth, he'll hold me in contempt like my mother-in-law. I choose the intermediary solution: my car is waiting to be cleared at the port.

H.H.'s house looks like him: bad taste on the inside, signs of new money on the outside. A soccer match is playing on television. We eat amid spectators' jeers. The boss and his two associates like soccer and H.H. pretends to be a fan. I'm the only one to express reservations about the sport. It's wrong of me, but I have never managed to be interested in competitive sports. I don't like crowds. I'm always afraid of getting trampled by frenzied masses. It's a fear my father passed on to me when I was small. He was afraid of demonstrations in the alleys of the medina in Fez. Naturally he was a patriot, but he kept his children from demonstrating. He was right. Our neighbor's son was crushed to death in the tanner's district. A martyr for the country's independence!

I tell myself it's lucky there's this match. It spares us having to find a topic of conversation. Will they return to the office or will they consider the inspection over? H.H. talks to them as if it were finished. He's right to do so. He knows the workings of the administration better than I do. I'm his boss but he leads. That's what my wife tells me. I hate giving orders. The only reason I have this job is because of my pile of degrees. He's proud that he didn't go to college.

The three men of the Commission return to the office with us, gather their belongings, and shake our hands. H.H. accompanies them out. He takes three bottles of Chivas from his drawer, placing each one in a plastic bag, then comes back, all smiles. We're both relieved.

"They're good people!" he tells me.

"So are we."

The *chaouch* announces another visitor. We look at one another. A beautiful brunette enters, walks up to H.H., and hands him a letter.

"He's the boss," he tells her.

Even this stranger spontaneously takes H.H. for the boss.

I don't look like a manager. I avoid looking her over the way some men do. I read her letter. She comes recommended by the undersecretary of state, whom I know nothing about. Her name is Doukkali, which doesn't suit her at all. H.H. asks her if she's related to Abdelwahab Doukkali, the singer.

"No relation," she murmurs.

She is tall, very properly dressed, and wearing little makeup; no doubt she's efficient. I ask her why she left her previous post. She answers me in a dry, crisp tone:

"The boss wanted to sleep with me... It was that or the door. I lodged a complaint against him for sexual harassment."

H.H. whistles in surprise.

"You think you're in Sweden?"

"No, I know where I am and what I'm doing. Morocco is changing. You'll see, I hope you'll come to the trial. . . as an observer, of course. Or perhaps as a witness."

The office is changing too. Before, we had Lalla Khadija for a secretary, a competent woman in her fifties, but a true representative of the old school: her French was riddled with Arabic words and she talked incessantly about her problems at home. Everyone knew the color of the upholstery in her living room, and she was always on the phone. We were getting complaints, so we installed a beeper to indicate when a new call was coming in. Now, with Miss Doukkali, it's the new generation. She's going to replace the other one during her sick leave.

I watch her when she isn't looking. She's well built. But no familiarity, nothing personal. H.H. doesn't like it. He thinks her presence will become irksome one of these days. At night we see her leave in a Fiat 127 driven by a young man who must be her brother or her fiancé.

I RING NAJIA'S BELL. ONCE AGAIN, HER MOTHER OPENS the door and gives me a warm welcome. She asks me in and, as usual, offers me tea and cakes. Smelling soup, I ask her for a bowl of *harira*. She's delighted that I appreciate her cooking. Najia won't be long; she's gone to the pediatrician. When she comes in with her daughter, she gives me a big smile and thanks me for stopping by. I can't tell if she's sincere. I wait until we're alone to clear things up. After dinner, I take her hand and ask her to marry me. She pulls it away and closes her eyes. I brush her lips and sense a sweetness that sends me back to my childhood. We could have something together, I think, but only if I stop what I have just barely begun, namely making my little deals. I promise her this. But how can I do it? Reject bribes, reverse the situation and pursue the corruptor? That would cause a scandal. I'd have to fight, and I'm not comfortable fighting. In any case, my decision is made. I'm determined not only to stop taking bribes, but to return the money I've already received.

Oddly enough, Najia is more worried about my honesty than about my conjugal entanglements. She knows it's over with Hlima. Time, habit, and fatigue have worn everything down. I have no more patience. All I have to do is give my wife and children three-quarters of my salary so they can live decently. Will Najia's salary be enough to live on? I don't dare ask; she's the one who takes her calculator from her briefcase and starts counting.

"I own the house. There's only the water and electricity to pay. I earn 4,852 DH a month and receive 1,202 DH from the bank as part of the indemnity from my husband's accident. The other part goes into an account in my daughter's name. My mother rents a house to a family in the medina and every three months the lawyer has to threaten to sue the people for their rent. That brings in about 1,000 DH a month after legal fees. All in all, I live well on about 7,000 DH a month. If you put in part of your salary, we'll have 10,000 DH.

*Corruption*

With that much money, we'll be almost middle class—but don't worry, we'll never really be. If you want to get married, start by getting divorced. Remember that the personal-status law allows you not only to take a second wife, but also to renounce the first. But you're a civilized man. You'll do the right thing without being unfair or cruel. I'll give you a month to take care of these matters. I'll be happy to make you happy, you know."

ALL MY LIFE, I HAVE BEEN CIVILIZED BUT POOR. I CAN'T help it. It's possible to be civilized, honest, and rich. The Koran encourages enterprising people who work and are involved in trade. In any case, God decides. He decided for my family long ago. We're poor from father to son. But God is not always with the poor. There's a Lebanese film with a title like that. It could also be the title of my story. It's a provocative title, though, and in times like these, with the blindness of the Islamists, I might get into trouble. In principle, God is with everyone. I can bear witness to that. Ever since I ceased to be an honest man, he has been placing obstacles in my path. This path hasn't been very long or complex, but at least I had nothing to be ashamed of. Right now I'm not on my usual path but at the intersection of several roads. I see a difficult road leading to a little house—Najia's house—where peace and even a little happiness are guaranteed.

On the other side, I see the same road I've been on forever, at the end of which are Hlima and the children. Strangely, they are not in a house but seated, all three in a red armchair on the sidewalk. There is no room for me. There is also a small middle road leading nowhere special, at the end of which Nadia has to put on false eyelashes while a singer on the television or radio belts out her despair at being alone. Putting false eyelashes on a dead eye! How strange. Donkeys are

87

passing back and forth through my field of vision. A parakeet is giving a speech and a cicada is eating the wires of the loudspeaker on top of the minaret.

THE NEW SECRETARY DOESN'T SAY A WORD. SHE DOES HER work, answers the phone, straightens her desk, and never comments on life in general or on the business at hand. Her behavior is surprising to us since the old secretary was always so curious. Maybe this one was sent as a spy? H.H. seems wary of her. He too talks less than before; when a private call comes in, he lowers his voice and offers to call back. It's impossible to sound her out or read anything in her face. You have to be wary of closed faces. Is she an undercover agent? H.H. thinks so; when Mr. Sabbane stops by unexpectedly, we choose to go out for coffee with him, far from indiscreet ears.

It's strange, even though I've taken only two commissions so far, I react like an expert in the field, like H.H., who must have amassed a healthy fortune in all the time he's been collecting his ten percent.

The press here is fairly silent about the great corruption hunt in Italy. Fortunately I stay informed by going to the French Cultural Center once a week and reading the foreign newspapers and magazines. Political party chiefs are resigning, deputies are losing their immunity, ministers are being prosecuted, top executives are committing suicide. Corruption is everywhere. What's different from us is that in Italy it concerns mostly leaders and takes place on a large scale. Although...

EVER SINCE I STOPPED TAKING THE BUS I FEEL BETTER. I feel less antipathy toward the human race. I even feel as if my countrymen are worthier than before; my opinion of them has gone up. I no longer have to shove up against them, endure their smells and bad moods. Public transportation does not encourage love for one's fellow human beings. When I was a child, my father rented out part of our house; we lived together, a sheet separating the two families. My mother didn't like it. These people were poorer than we were and, most importantly, didn't have the same upbringing. They were peasants. I didn't like the smells from their cooking. They had three children who cried too much. It was a dismal time, ill-preparing me to tolerate my peers.

THE WHITE SPOTS ARE SPREADING TO THE BACK OF MY hand, my forearm, and forehead. I'm turning white. People look at me with concern; they feel sorry for me. I'm losing the natural color of my skin as I run through the dirty money. I'm my own dirty money laundering machine. The problem is you can see it, though I may be the only one to make the connection. Other people must figure it's an illness due to a psychological shock or a major disturbance. My eyebrows are awash in this wave of whiteness. It looks like makeup. Is it contagious, dangerous? I'll have to see a specialist, whom I guess I'll have to pay with dirty money, but he won't know. It's a way of curing evil with evil.

Without even examining me, the doctor says:

"It's a vitiligo, a simple pigmentation problem. Nothing serious. It's a poor distribution of pigment. The white parts are deprived of pigment while there is a large quantity in the unaffected areas. It's not very pretty, but it's not dangerous. That said, we have to do a few tests, because I also notice some red marks... Bad circulation."

Several days later, I return with the tests. He reads them, looking up at me from time to time. He purses his lips and says "Oh!... That's strange... That's rare," then stands up, takes off his glasses, and asks me:

"What line of work are you in?"

"I'm an engineer."

"That's an envied position, I suppose."

"I don't know."

"Tell me, have you ever had any grafts?"

"Grafts of what?"

"An organ?... I say that because a strange thing is happening. Your vitiligo is accompanied by an allergy, a kind of rejection."

"Yes, I see. Tell me, is there a treatment?"

"No, as you get used to it you won't pay attention to it anymore. Sometimes the pigmentation returns to normal. It's psychosomatic. You must be overemotional. Look on the bright side of life. Do what everyone does. Let your blood flow easily. Don't trouble it with too many upsetting thoughts."

"What thoughts?"

"You must think too much."

"Perhaps."

Then I tell him I've been constipated for some time.

"You should have told me sooner. It's all coming clear. You're retaining instead of excreting. You have a guilty conscience. You need relaxation. Take up a sport."

"Is that all I can do?"

"Increase your flexibility."

"Are there evening courses for that?"

"At all hours. Morning and evening, day and night. Let yourself go. Let life pamper you..."

I've got to change the other dollars. Since I'm leaving home, I'll give Hlima a good chunk of money. Her frown the other day upon discovering my vitiligo says a lot about her humanity. She has no pity. If I try to touch her, I'm sure she'll push me away. She's afraid of illness. She never visits a sick person. She boycotts sickness hoping she'll be spared. Only after two years of marriage did I realize my wife was neurotic. She adapts well to her psychological problems in that she doesn't place much importance on them. I was bothered by her fixations, irritated by her indifference, and I found her obsession with money and material comfort intolerable. And yet, I produced two children and traveled a long way with her. It's all far from logical. I've always thought that men were cowards, especially where women are concerned. I've wasted a lot of time. Unfortunately, I woke up too late.

Am I free? Yes, of course. I like the expression "free as the wind." I too can go anywhere, wherever I want. I can stop in at one of those seedy bistros where they play cards. I'll order a beer and drink it while eating steamed fava beans. I'll comment on yesterday's soccer match and bad-mouth the Americans who are bombarding Baghdad.

Yes, I'm free. I can go for a walk or a taxi ride along the corniche, smoke a cigarette while thinking of Najia, have my shoes shined, buy a book, eat roasted pumpkin seeds, count the number of passersby, remember the number of those dressed in white and forget those in gray, guess their professions, whether they're married or not, whether they have jobs or not. I can even climb a large rock on the breakwater and look out at the sea, alone, my back to the city, stare at a seagull and follow its flight, to the point of forgetting the vitiligo and the constipation. I am free to eat prunes to relieve the constipation, though my stomach no longer obeys. I can also let myself slip slowly down the big rock and join the waves. I don't know how to swim and I'm afraid of falling into the exact spot where the city sewers let out. It stinks. I'm free to forget that it stinks. To float away with other people's shit is indecent. I'm not even talking about being fancy. No, I'm better than that: I shouldn't think so badly of myself. I know I'm entirely free to act and think, and no one can stop me from thinking and dreaming, my only freedom. I'm armored; my dreams are impenetrable and I alone possess the key. I don't even need to hide it, it's in my head. There is no one to stop me from acting… No one? I see Wassit and Karima's faces. I see Najia's silhouette in the background. No, I'm not free. I'll do nothing of the sort. I'll forget everything. I'll slowly head home, where Hlima is waiting for me with her messy hair, her eyes swollen from crying, her bitterness, her wretched accusations, and her anger ready to explode.

I'll return home and think of nothing. I'll stuff my ears with earplugs, pick up a book and fall asleep reading. I'll sit in a little corner of the living room or lock myself in the kitchen. I'll be in peace. This is freedom, my freedom, this and nothing more. It's cramped and small, but this is it.

Now that I'm aware of the disaster, I don't know what to do. Yesterday, my mother-in-law came to see me at the office. It's the second time she's pulled this on me. The first time was when Karima was born. My son was three years old. She had decided to surprise her daughter by secretly organizing Karima's baptism and Wassit's circumcision. Hlima wasn't to know a thing. This is common in wealthier families; my mother-in-law couldn't resist the chance to make that point, and especially to harp on my less-than-modest salary. The generosity of rich people is often suspect. They are incapable of discretion. At the time, I didn't hold it against her since I didn't know her well. Her visit yesterday had a different objective: to reconcile me with Hlima. Oddly enough, she was unusually restrained, even critical of her daughter. She said she understood me and was only thinking of Wassit and Karima, that for her, money was just soot and that there was more to life than material comfort. "Health is the only thing that matters. No health, no money. A healthy body and mind is what we must ask of God. The rest will come later.

Without health there's no happiness, no joy, no future..."
I was surprised. I barely recognized her. She must be sick, I told myself. She must feel her end is near.

I calmly told her that I had no intention of making up with Hlima, that the gulf between us was too deep. She left disgruntled, pausing to take a dig at me: "God will be your judge! I'll leave you in his hands."

Since then, I've been in God's hands and am feeling pretty good. H.H. looks at me sympathetically. He's not familiar with this sort of problem: to be truly in God's hands! What a windfall! I'm going to take advantage of it to ask for a little more justice and an improvement in my daily life. I don't need much: a raise in my salary, more commissions for Hlima, for Karima to get well. Her asthma is complicated. The doctor spoke to me about a stay at a specialized center. He thinks her breath is going to get shorter and shorter; her left lung is in bad shape as well. The doctor is one of my brothers-in-law. Our relationship is cordial, nothing more. He doesn't charge me for visits, a fact that my mother-in-law already pointed out to me. How does it benefit them to humiliate the poor? They think it's my fault I have no money. I haven't been able to adapt to my surroundings. I haven't thought it worthwhile to make a few compromises. The doctor doesn't say so but he must think it. We don't see one another socially. Hlima and I don't go out much at night because we don't have a car. Getting a taxi at night in Casablanca is quite an ordeal, so we decline our rare dinner invitations, except when it's an obligation, a wedding or a funeral.

When the doctor called this morning I got scared. It's the first time he's called me. He was thinking about Karima and gave me the address of a place I should send her; he added that it would cost me between ten and fifteen thousand dirhams. He also said he would help me get a discount, since the director of the clinic is a friend. First, Karima needs to calm her asthma; then we'll take it from there.

I PUT DOWN THE PHONE AND WIPE MY BROW AND forehead. I'm breaking into a cold sweat. I leave the office and rush home. The taxi gets caught in a traffic jam. I get out and continue on foot. At home, Hlima is sewing. She's surprised to see me in this state. I ask where Karima is.

"She's in school. Why?"

"Is she okay?"

"Yes, except that the other night she had an asthma attack while you were out with one of your tarts."

"Let's not mix things up."

"Fortunately Dr. Saïd was here. He gave her a shot."

"That's just it, he called me at the office and told me she had to be hospitalized."

"Yes, I know. But with what money?"

"The money? I'll find the money."

I LOCK MYSELF IN THE BATHROOM AND BREAK OPEN MY piggy bank, *Being and Nothingness*. I count the bills. Ten hundred-dollar bills, and over 2,500 DH. That'll be enough to start. After that I'll borrow or ask H.H. whether a document needs to be signed. The dollars need to be changed. I go back to the same branch that already changed part of the sum for me. The teller recognizes me right away, smiles, and asks me to follow him. I find myself in front of a manager, perhaps the head of the branch.

"Do you have more dollars to change?" he asks immediately.

"Yes. That's why I came."

He skims a file as he speaks to me.

"I was going to write to you to propose an investment for this money. But since you're here, there's no need for the letter."

The teller adds: "And as the proverb says, 'When there's water for ablutions there's no point using the stone!'"

He holds out his hand and I give him the ten hundred-dollar bills. He counts and recounts them and verifies the numbers.

"These are brand-new bills from the same series. That's a problem."

I look at him, astonished.

"Where did you get these dollars?" asks the manager.

"It's none of your business."

"I know, but in a little while this question will be put to you in a different fashion, in different places, and, most importantly, by different people. Better to tell me the truth. This series, from L56061450A to L56062000A, is highly sought after at the moment, and not by a collector! Last time, you changed ten bills from L560561450A to L56061460A, and, as if by some miracle, today's bills follow up to 70A. So, are you going to tell me where this money's from and who gave it to you?"

I feel like answering, like in a scene from a bad movie, "My American uncle!"

But this man doesn't look easygoing. Maybe he's a police officer passing himself off as the branch manager. Faced with my surprise and silence, he makes a call.

"I think we're on the right track," I hear him say.

I stand up to take a few steps, but the teller forces me to sit down.

"Give me back my money."

"Sorry, it's not your money. This money was stolen, perhaps by you, perhaps by the person who gave it to you. That makes you either a thief or a fence. And that'll get you four to five years in prison."

Then after a silence, he lowers his voice and says:

"If you want, we can make a deal. For the moment, we three

are the only ones who know about this. You decide whether this delicate matter will remain between us, a private affair, our little secret. Sometimes you have to know how to lose in life."

He's crazy! Who does he think he's talking to? I've spent my life not winning. I wasn't exactly losing, because my hyperactive honesty prevented me from taking any risks. The one time I make a few pennies, someone wants to take them from me! It's not fair. There's no justice for the poor. Power and honesty don't mix. I can already see myself: handcuffed, facing one of those inspectors specializing in strong-arm interrogations. "We have forty-eight hours to make you confess," he'll tell me with a smile. "You're lucky the close watch has been reduced. Before, we had all the time in the world to do our jobs. Today, with these human-rights leagues and the chatterbox national and foreign press, we have to work fast. That's democracy for you: a question of time. In less than forty-eight hours we have to accomplish what we used to do calmly over a week or two!"

I LOOK UP AND OBSERVE THE BLOATED FACE OF THIS blackmailer-thief who is entirely capable of handing me over to the police. I have a moment of doubt. How can he possibly accuse me like this? Is it because he can read everything on my face? Honest people don't know how to lie. As soon as they stray from the straight path, everyone knows it. They give themselves away, no need to denounce them. Except that in my case, I'm sure someone alerted the two men from the bank. Who? Mr. Sabbane or H.H.? But why? Out of vengeance? Out of spite, pure and simple? I realize now how many deals my honesty, my lack of flexibility, my lack of a conciliatory spirit prevented from going through and enriching H.H. and his accomplices. He must have pushed me to taste easy money, just so I would have an idea of what I caused him to lose. What perversion! What sadism! What's more, if I'm arrested, he's the one who'll replace me. They're all in this together: Sabbane, my assistant, the bank agents, and perhaps even certain police officers and inspectors. Add to that Hlima and her mother, and the picture is complete. Maybe it's a bluff. I should never have accepted foreign money... I should never have accepted money, of any sort! Now, what should I do? Leave them some? Object and end up face-to-face with the police in a damp cell? I'll never be able to explain this money. I'm caught, like an animal in a trap. If I so much as agree to make a deal it boils down to an admission of guilt. I'm corrupt, newly corrupt, but what do the date and nature of the first offense matter?

I stand, take a few steps in the office, smoke a cigarette and look out the window at the city. I love looking at life from behind a window. I imagine the beauty and joy, I guess at the pain and unhappiness of the people passing by. This woman in the sky-blue djellaba riding on an old motorbike, her child behind her, must be happy. She's probably as poor as I am but she's not cornered like me at this moment. The young man with his back to the wall is peacefully enjoying the sun and no longer expects a job offer despite his law degree. I envy him too. But the man who is running with the fat briefcase must not be happy. He's perspiring; he stops, runs his hand over his bald spot, and wipes off the sweat. He must not live a good life. A little like me. A couple of tourists stop and take a picture. The man is very tall, the woman too. They are handsome and happy. They must not have any worries. They're not locked up in an office in the process of negotiating a deal to change their dollars! When will I too be a respected tourist, with dirhams I can change for dollars in New York or San Francisco? I think of Karima and Wassit again. They're far from imagining their father caught in a trap, on a dead-end street. They don't deserve this. I give in. I stop thinking, stop weighing the pros and cons. I give up. Do I have a choice? No one to advise me, to help me and support me. I'm alone. I can make out my image in the window; it looks slightly contorted. It's the heat, the anxiety, the fear. I've never been very handsome, but the cheap glass is distorting my face. My eyes are fooling me. My sight is going, it's true, but it's also playing tricks on me. The face in the window moves from right to left. I remain still. The window is slightly ajar and the wind makes my image shiver. If I could, I'd go right out the window, disappear like smoke. That would leave my blackmailers in a pickle! They would have to explain my disappearance to the judge, while I would attend their trial, invisible. That would be my revenge. The door opens. The window slams. I turn around and find myself facing an unshaven, menacing hulk. Now there are three of them wishing me ill. The hulk pushes me down into the chair. He says he's an undercover agent and that he's sent important people to prison. He's talking nonsense. They're trying to intimidate and scare me. I resist with my silence; what's the use of talking to brutes? I have always dreamed of being an urban Tarzan, a man of justice, a savior. I feel my muscles. They're awfully thin. I'm short of breath. I always knew that cigarettes would hasten my end. If the colossus punches me, I'll faint. When I was in the army, I often claimed to be sick and avoided the tiring exercises. I locked myself in the infirmary and read. My delicate health was a pretext for enjoying a bit of solitude. I hated living in close quarters with other men. Now here I am, surrounded by three brutes whose breathes smells of garlic and beer. This has to stop, I have to break it up. Immediately. Right away. Without further delay. I have to get out of here, right now. I'm suffocating. I feel nauseous, especially when they lean over me and their bad breath makes my head spin. Now. I will it. I will that they stop this ordeal. What if I burned all the dollars? That would get them! And if I set the entire room on fire? Difficult to do. It's an

Corruption

order. Right away. Immediately. I must get up and slap each of
them a few times. They must cry and beg me on their knees.
No, that's not me. That's someone else. I hate seeing a man on
his knees. Give 'em a kick in the behind, or in the groin. A
kick in the balls is awful. At once a strong and muffled pain.
They'd be all doubled over, calling for help. I'd take advantage
of the moment to make my getaway and run along the shore,
yelling, singing, ripping up dollars and feeding the gulls. But
such is the world. Power goes to those who make indifference
a virtue, who spurn others, leaving them to die merciless
deaths, unconsoled and misunderstood. I am thinking right
now of my friend O., whom I saw the other day in his hospital bed. Life was going on around him but death was there as
well. It was taunting him as the nurse placed a tube just under
his lung to extract liters of water and blood. He felt relief when
almost three liters of liquid were removed that had been
pressing on his lung and preventing him from breathing. He's
a very close friend but he lives far from Casablanca. I hadn't
seen him for a year and we were reunited in this awful room.
My problems seemed so small as I watched him while he was-
n't looking and imagined death caressing his forehead and
squeezing his neck.

Look! Yet another man hitting a child. The kid is learning
violence at his own expense; he too may strike his father or
even his mother one day. No one stops to prevent the man from
assaulting him. It may be his son or his servant boy. I make a
gesture with my hand as if to protest and express my power-
lessness. The three men surround and threaten me. I sit down
again and ask for my dollars back. The banker hands them to
me willingly. I count them. Ten stinking bills. I crumple them
up, bend down as if to pick something up and quickly set them
on fire with my lighter. One of the three men rushes over
screaming and stamps on the bills. He salvages a few of them.

I stand up, a free man, while the insults pour from the three stinking mouths. I head for the door and no one stops me from leaving. Outside, the weather is warm. I take off my jacket, undo my tie and walk slowly, blending into the crowd, which seems quite bustling this morning.

Like a character in a book, I have arrived at a particular place in my life and hesitate between fighting or destroying myself. I am incapable of destroying others. The prospect of fighting, of a new battle, frightens me. Suicide is not within the realm of possibility. It's a question one rarely asks oneself. There are depressed people around me but no suicides. When I was in high school, my history professor, a Frenchman doing his alternative military service, hung himself, which was quite a shock to us. He'd corrected our homework, returned it to us, and established order in the classroom. The next day we waited for him. I was fourteen. I have to admit that I cried. Later I learned that his wife had cheated on him and he couldn't stand the humiliation.

I walk without hurrying and feel a sudden burst of clarity. I can't see myself being ushered into the darkness of a damp cell. Nor can I imagine prison. No, you have to speak out against everything—speak out while walking, while talking, while sleeping, while dreaming, while creating, pushing yourself to the point of madness; it's freedom, not a sickness. People bump into me and no one apologizes. The fact that I'm a tired-looking man inspires no respect. I know that people don't have the time to look into my soul and see that I'm a good person. They couldn't care less, and they're right. H.H. doesn't even have a soul, and yet he is treated respectfully. No one is disrespectful of me, but I'm ignored. I don't exist. That's what I should have said to the three brutes in the bank: "You have before you someone who doesn't exist. It's a vision. It's the wind." They probably would have hit me just to prove to me that I do exist. But I don't need proof. I could take my life, cancel it out. It's easy to say. Do I still have the courage to face my children? Will they be ashamed of me? The white spots have disappeared from the back of my right hand, but they linger on my forehead and behind my ears. I'm sure they'll go away in time.

It's been a long time since I've mixed in with the crowds. "Choose your death," a voice tells me, "here, now, in this crowd, at this intersection, facing this beggar who looks at you with watery eyes, here in the presence of this beautiful woman, a foreigner come for the exoticism and passion of the unknown, choose your death and, if you can, cross the street, cross the city line and even the border, go far, as far as your means allow, descend into Africa or head up to Europe, be alive and determined; you're not soiled because you took a lousy commission, no, you're soiled because you let yourself get caught in a trap, and you struggle with shadows who have no scruples; choose silence, then, and settle into its abyss, there where no light will blind you."

Another voice, no doubt Najia's, speaks to me softly: "It's not too late to work it all out. You'll get rid of the dirty money, change jobs, and we'll build a life together. You're convinced that your assistant sold you out, but if you don't react, he'll go even further. Where does this apathy come from? You don't react when you need to; you wait and miss your chance to win. Your destiny is in your hands now. It's not too late…"

I STEP INSIDE THE CENTRAL CAFÉ. SOME MEN ARE PLAYING cards, others dominoes. Some are pretending to read the newspaper as children polish their shoes. I too pick up a newspaper and scan it. It's poorly written, poorly laid out, poorly informed, poorly everything. I throw it on the seat. A hand picks it up and opens it to the crossword puzzle. I drink a glass of tea and watch the passersby. There are still too many beggars in this city. It's the effect of the drought; they come from the country. "They fall instead of rain," the waiter tells me, forgetting that he too was a shepherd five years ago. The shoe-shine boys sell American cigarettes by the piece. They're police informers. They don't have much to tell, but you never know, you need ears everywhere. I recognize one of the members of the inspection commission. He's walking next to a woman in a djellaba; it could be his wife or his mother. I look at my watch. Time to go back to the office. H.H. must be worried. I won't tell him about the bank episode. I'll let him come to me. His friends will fill him in. I'll know if he's an accomplice or not.

At the office, the new secretary is all excited. As soon as she sees me, she runs up and tells me that the inspectors have come back. I calm her down. She's worried because she's being accused of having stolen an old typewriter. She protests, on the verge of tears. H.H. isn't here. He's gone to see the director. As soon as I sit down, one of the members of the commission, the little fat one, comes and gives me a paper to sign. I read it. A confirmation of their visit. Nothing serious.

An hour later, the director calls me in.

"You're suspended and accused of embezzling public property. The court will inform you of this soon. I thought it my duty to warn you and am taking this opportunity to express my sympathy. You have always been a good citizen and an excellent civil servant. But we all have our weaknesses. Now you will have to pay."

"Pay for what?"

"Your wayward behavior. You are accused of having stolen office equipment and selling it in the old flea market at Jouteya."

"It's a mistake, sir. I never sold anything at Jouteya."

"If you're innocent, so much the better. All you have to do is prove it. I have nothing against you, but I'm responsible for everything found in this building—the chairs, the typewriters, the pens, and the people as well. If they tell me that one of my subordinates sold a typewriter, I'm obliged to take action. It's only natural. That typewriter belongs to the state, it's public property purchased with taxpayers' money, which is to say the people's money."

"But I borrowed the typewriter, I didn't steal it."

"Maybe. But you had forty-eight hours from the moment the inspectors realized it was gone to bring it back, and the inspectors came by two months ago. You'll have to explain all that to them. They're not brutes. Have confidence in your country's justice system."

I WOULD SO LIKE TO HAVE CONFIDENCE, BUT THE DIE IS cast in advance, the game is rigged. I must pay to set an example. It had to be me. That's the way it always goes, as my father would have said. You're punished for being poor; and you're poor because you're honest; honest because you've been taught by your father to respect the law. An old typewriter, a 1960 Olivetti! A collector's item! They're hateful. I'm going to give it back right away, but they won't want it. It's only a pretext. I leave the director's office disgusted but not despairing. I understand now, but it's too late to change my attitude and behavior. Since I'm suspended, there's no point in returning to my desk. My job is suspended, and my salary too. My signature is now worth nothing. Before, it was estimated in the tens of thousands. Today, zero. It doesn't open any doors. From now on I'm a free man, a brand-new man. I have a few bills left.

I'm back on the street again. I stop at a barber shop and ask him to wash my hair and shave me. I look at myself in the mirror and it seems as if the white spots are less obvious than

before. It's funny to have half your eyebrows all white. Why
do barbers hang their certificates? This one's name is Omar.
His identity photo is surrounded by a series of flags: he must
have participated in an international competition in Toulouse.
Over the Israeli flag he has done a bad job of gluing a
Palestinian one. You can see Israel clearly sticking out. He must
have been criticized for participating in the competition. The
radio is playing a monotonous song that hurts my ears. While
tending to my hair, he is talking to someone behind him, working at an angle. All I want is to take my mind off things. Now
he's done; I pay and leave. Suddenly a stocky, elegant man
passes me and does a double take. I look at him too and think
I recognize Tajeddine, the son of my primary school teacher.
He speaks up first. We haven't seen each other in twenty-five
years. Very well dressed, stout; class and money. He kisses and
hugs me and tells me how happy he is to see me. Strangely, he
addresses me formally. I use informal address right away. He
invites me for a drink and picks the café. "Not here. We're
going to the coast, to my hotel in Ryad Salam."

We get into his limousine and the chauffeur takes off. I'm
happy about this encounter. I'm not going to ruin his pleasure
by telling him that I just lost my job and am being sued for
embezzling public property! He tells me about his companies
in America and England. He has no qualms about telling
me that he's made a fortune simply by following his instincts.
I followed mine too, and look where it got me! I tell him that
instinct has to be accompanied by something else. He smiles
and places his finger on his forehead. Intelligence! I'm
intelligent too but I don't travel in a Mercedes 500 with a
chauffeur. We have a drink by the hotel pool and he tells me
about his life since he left Morocco. He started from scratch,
and now commands a large fortune. He's become American,
not on paper but in his head. He talks efficiency, profitability,

industry, seriousness, adventure, risk, integration... He
paints a portrait of the American that makes me laugh, using
every cliché in the book. Maybe they're not clichés. He's
returned to this country to invest but deplores people's lack
of seriousness.

"You see, my time is precious," he tells me, "and here, everywhere I go they make me wait. Moroccans inherited sluggish-
ness from the French. It's too bad. Money in itself isn't
interesting, it's a symbol. What's exciting is not possessing it,
but varying the methods of earning it. Anyone can get rich. But
to be stronger than money, that not everyone can attain. I was
poor, you remember, and I've been rich, and I've gone
bankrupt several times. Money is only a symbol. Here, people
stupidly display their wealth. Money must never be an end in
itself. It's a means, a symbol, I tell you!"

After talking about himself for an hour, he asks me what I've
been doing.

"I work at the Ministry of Development. Right now I'm on
sick leave. I'm resting."

He offers to take me with him to New York for a checkup.
His treat. Is he joking? Maybe not? People who have made a
fortune often try to be useful; it's as if they want to be for-
given their success. I feel like taking him up on it and going
with him to America. I could be his secretary but I don't speak
English. Too bad, otherwise I would have gone for it. This is all
nonsense. I too tried to have a little of the symbol; it didn't
really work for me. I get up to leave; he stops me and insists
I must have lunch with him.

"I have to tell my family," I say.

He takes a telephone from his briefcase and asks me the
number.

"I don't have a telephone. I requested one three years ago.
No lines."

"I'll send my chauffeur to tell your wife you've been detained."

"No, don't bother."

He invites me to the Cabestan. The fish is fresh, the cooking is light, and the French wine excellent. I eat like a child. With a good platter of seafood in front of me, I forget the world and its troubles, my problems and pain. We drink. We laugh. We toast our rekindled friendship several times. It's joy and happiness. He stops talking about America but I still don't mention what happened to me. He gives me several business cards. He has several telephones, fax machines, and addresses. He adds a telephone number by hand and tells me:

"You can reach me anywhere, anytime, when you dial this number; it finds me. That's progress, incredible. It's a private number, and, in addition, if you add this code, I pay for the call. So, it's all set, you'll call me!"

WHAT WILL I CALL TO TELL HIM? THAT I'M ON THE EDGE of a precipice, that I'm tempted by suicide? My troubles and grief with Hlima and the ignoble H.H.? There isn't much symbolism there! I put the cards in my pocket. He tells his chauffeur to take me wherever I want and returns to the hotel for a nap.

I climb into the luxury car, the cigar almost finished, and ask him to drive along the corniche. Between the alcohol and the cigar, I have a feeling of being elsewhere, on a cloud, far from Casablanca and its problems. I'm a bit drunk. I feel good and know that the fall will be hard. My American friend must be snoring now while his magic phone number searches for him in the depths of a dream that takes place in the medina in the fifties, when we played with marbles and tops. After the ride by the shore, I ask the chauffeur to drop me on Oran Street.

No one is home. I fall asleep on the sofa.

MY AMERICAN FRIEND WAS ONLY PASSING THROUGH. NOW he's far away. I too am far from everything, from my work, my responsibilities, my conscience and myself. I feel like a stranger to everything. To be a stranger to oneself is very handy. Like that other stranger, I could commit a crime in the sun and be none the worse for it. Except that my mother is still alive and expecting me to visit her in the old house in the medina of Fez, where everything is collapsing, where the stones form a crumbling heap. Fez is a wound. Every time I follow the road to the medina, I feel an old anger well up inside me. The city of my childhood has a deformed body and a tired soul. It's good for tourists, who go into raptures over the poor artisan pretending to work the copper. They shoot movies there set in the Middle Ages, or in any case in the past. I feel as much a stranger there as I do right now. It's lucky no one is home. I need to be alone. I would be incapable of talking or of answering questions.

I go into Karima's room and look for the typewriter. I can't find it. Nor in Wassit's room. It's disappeared. Maybe Hlima threw it out. Ah—here she is now with the children. I say nothing. I stay huddled on the sofa. The children kiss me and go to their rooms. Hlima looks me over with a worried eye. She tells me they were at her nephew's circumcision. I couldn't care less about the ceremony and make no reply. I mustn't comment, whatever I do. I could spoil everything by talking. I'm not always in control of myself. Sometimes I say horrible things that I don't really think and then it takes months to erase them. Better to be silent. It's more prudent and sometimes more effective. I ask Hlima where the typewriter is. She tells me she's used it to prop up Wassit's bed. The box spring lost a leg. She reminds me that it's completely rusted and unusable. I go into Wassit's room and bend down. On top of the typewriter is an old Larousse dictionary, which creates the balance necessary to support the bed.

AS I STAND UP, I NOTICE THAT LITTLE PIECES OF PAPER full of words are coming out of the bowels of the typewriter. I move closer and notice that between the old dictionary and the old typewriter a hollow has been carved out in the shape of a vertical tube; letters pass through which the machine gathers into words and even sentences. It's magic. I sit on the floor and begin collecting the little slips of paper. A certain order must be followed to make sentences: "The cicadas never enter the wake of tears..." "China is near," "The castle lay down on a bed of ferns," "The sun and the rain in the schoolmaster's fez..." "Our need for consolation is insatiable." I smile and leave the typewriter to write its stories. There is no longer any question of giving it back. Now that objects are taunting and communicating with us, nothing serious can happen to me. It is no doubt because the typewriter is inhabited by an evil genie that the inspectors want it back. Maybe one day it will start making real banknotes; the dictionary has only to pour in a bunch of numbers. It will be the typewriter that types the golden letters.

I AM SUDDENLY OVERWHELMED BY AN UNUSUAL drowsiness. I have to get away for a few hours, as far as possible without turning around to see if anyone is following me. I am dropping with weariness and fatigue. It's as if I wanted it this way. I'm not here. I'm not responsible. I'm not the one you see. I'm no one. It's easy to be no one. All you have to do is go to Cairo or Calcutta and blend into the crowd. There I would be a lost foreigner, one among millions of men, a being of no importance. I could lose myself in Calcutta, the typewriter under my arm. People would think that I was an itinerant letter writer, a journalist on assignment. They would say nothing to me. They would let me croak in peace, on a corner of the sidewalk. I would be neither the first nor the last.

An old yellow truck would collect my corpse, still hugging the typewriter, the object of my misfortune and my salvation, and throw them in a common grave.

I'll have to confront those petty bosses, answer their questions, pretend to listen to them and endure their sarcasm and cruelty. I don't know if I'll appear before the disciplinary committee or before the judge. It depends on management. I'm a smoke screen and I know it. It's clear. I have always been a smoke screen because of my obsession with being honest. But what does management want? To prove that it is honest and that it hunts down and punishes those who steal from the state? I can tell them until I'm blue in the face that I only borrowed this typewriter, which was no longer being used, that they should even thank me since it was blocking the hallway. How many times did H.H. trip over it! Once he even got his toe stuck between the *A* and the *Z*. The letters had bitten him — after all, he'd kicked it. Let's get back to management's ulterior motives: my presence in this office doesn't suit the City Council of Walaya. I am not a modern man, I do not keep up with the times, and I prevent those around me from benefiting from these times and its goodies. I'm the one who keeps the machine from running. That's why, it seems, they call me the "grain of sand," like my friend in Tangier. But where is justice? It's precisely in the name of justice that I am now being accused of embezzling public property! When I explain to Najia that I'm wanted by the state because of an old typewriter, she won't believe me. She'll say I'm lying to hide the true motive for the accusation: corruption of a state worker. I would have thought the same thing. But it's not the case. It would be best for me to talk to her about it right away, immediately. A kind of crazy impatience is eating at me. I put my head under the cold-water faucet and stay there a few minutes. When I was little I thought that by washing my head I was also washing my thoughts. The bad ideas and dark thoughts would be driven away by the shampoo. I was convinced of this and felt better afterwards. Today I like to feel the coolness of the water in my hair, and I don't believe that anything or anyone will chase away the clutter that makes my head so heavy.

Najia is watching her daughter do her homework when I arrive. I don't want to bother them. I sit down in the living room and read the newspaper. It's so badly written, it's appalling. I look inside at the miscellaneous news items. After all, my case would fit in there. It's not political, it's not criminal. What is it exactly? Minor delinquency? Misappropriation? Embezzlement? Corruption? It's really more "vengeance." Unfortunately, there is no such category. So many cases could fall into it! Someone should start a newspaper for the small honest minority—it deserves it. Because it isn't enough to be honest; you have to forever be proving you're not a thief. We should form a union or a corporation to defend our unwavering standards and our honor. They're capable of infiltrating the movement and getting us to elect a treasurer who would walk away with the kitty! One more perversion.

I remember the day burglars broke into our house while we were away. They sawed through the window bars, broke the glass, and made off with my mother's jewelry, a radio, a chandelier, the telephone, and even some ashtrays. When my father went to the police station to lodge a complaint, they kept him there for hours. The people passing by who saw him sitting on a bench in the hallway took pity on him and said, "God is merciful!" When he finally met with the officer in charge of registering his complaint, he was questioned about his life, his business, his children, everything but the burglary. He got up and explained to the policeman that there had been a mistake, that he was not the burglar but the victim, and he left. No report was made. When he got home, he told us: "In this country, thieves are protected, the corrupt are encouraged, and honest people are threatened!"

I throw away the newspaper. At least Najia smiled when she looked at me. She's a good woman. She has succeeded in maintaining a balance in her difficult life; I admire her, but I don't know if I love her. She soothes me, even if she sometimes shakes me up. I also think of Hlima, her scheming, her pettiness.

I start imagining, and I imagine her. It's what I do best. Imagine until I feel others' pain, make it my own, add my own tears and get back up like a child after a fall. I imagine Hlima without me, free forever of this husband incapable of making her proud and filling her eyes with the sites of the world. I see her sorting through the closet, filling a laundry bin with my old shirts with the worn collars, my two suits, my outdated ties, and my shoes that have been patched several times. I imagine her ridding the drawers of everything that could remind her of my existence. I imagine her tired, crying, her head resting on the sewing table, cursing life and the fate that cast her into the arms of a worthy but poor and ambitionless man. I imagine her telling the children some sort of nonsense story like: "He fell into the trap of a witch who took him from us... Now he has to beg outside mosques. Your father is an irresponsible man. He abandoned us to follow a prostitute who must have made him drink an evil potion. He lost his memory and no longer recognizes anyone. He's lost everything, his job, his honor and his dignity. He's dead. Or rather it would be better for us if he were. Even if he comes back, he'll be a different man. Luckily my mother sends us enough to live on..."

I imagine her covering with a black cloth the part of the photograph in which I appear, changing the sheets to get rid of my scent, tampering with the memories in which we were happy. I am speaking as if I were already on the other side.

I am speaking and chasing away images that I see too clearly not to believe in them. I imagine my mother-in-law heaving a sigh of relief, mentally calculating how much this unexpected absence is going to cost her. I see her talking it over with her sons-in-law, who prefer to play cards while pretending to listen. Their lives are settled: simple and efficient, corrupt and carefree, selfish and happy. They talk about the drop in real estate values and the stability of the dirham. They talk about Europe and how they don't understand what's gotten into the Italian justice system. All these industrialists and politicians accused of corruption and thrown in prison! It's suicidal, one of them says. It's a bluff, says the other. I imagine them comfortable with their bodies, which they care for as best they can. For them, I don't exist. I am not a member of the family. I am just the husband of a woman who was foolish enough to make a mistake in her youth, and therefore must pay. That's all. They don't even know where I work or what I do. I'm a pathetic little salaried man who doesn't even enter their field of vision. What might I do in this glorious field of vision? Play tennis or golf, collect the balls, clean the lawn, serve drinks, watch the cars? Ultimately they'd give me one of those copper badges car attendants pin on their gray smocks to distinguish themselves from the unlicensed beggars who ask for handouts anywhere and from anyone. Yes, when they do good, they make sure you know it. Humiliating people comes naturally; it goes without saying that they're not going to get hung up on the case of a man of no importance, a man who thinks, acts, makes mistakes, and falls like a wounded animal. Everything has been planned out by them or by their parents long ago. First of all be on guard, cover yourself, protect the rear, and then, from time to time, you can look right and left, dig a small coin from your pocket and give it to the man on the ground. There are plenty of men of no importance cluttering the sidewalks and alleyways. Give out of fear of God, fear of ending up on a bench in the cold and the rain, one day when life is no longer life, when a grain of sand has clogged the works, fear of having to join the band of corpses, their shrouds eaten by rats, infinitely awaiting the final judgment day. They see themselves thrown one on top of the other like sacks of flour, their souls gone but their eyes and ears open. Then they give, recite two or three prayers, and continue along their way. All I do is watch. And I see beyond what is visible. Sometimes I guess, I imagine, I invent just a little.

Do I need a looking glass to see what awaits me? Anything is possible. Hlima could change her attitude and start defending me madly, passionately. She might, for once, calculate correctly, say the necessary words, make the long-awaited gesture. She who loves melodrama on television could act out one to save her unjustly accused husband. What am I being accused of, in fact? "Embezzlement of public property"! I borrowed a rusty old typewriter in which a spider had woven its web. Is that public property? Administratively, yes. The typewriter exists in the inventory, it is recorded on page 32 of the complete equipment ledger. Everything is there, even the staples, the pencil sharpeners, the blotters. It's true I borrowed the typewriter (with no intention of keeping it!) because it was serving no purpose and blocking the hall. Then I forgot it existed. Karima didn't use it; the keys were jammed with rust. She played with it until she got tired of it. But the judges would laugh at all these details, which would only weaken my case.

Everyone knows that this is not the true motive. For twenty years I resisted, fighting alone and with all my strength against corruption and its temptations. I caused my family to lead a life of poverty. We all suffered, but our consciences were clear. I caved in twice. I took two commissions. I touched dirty money and was invaded by white spots. Now these spots are going away. The money burned my fingers. It wreaked havoc in my life, destroyed my illusions, ravaged my sleep. And here I am being charged with a misdemeanor!

I imagine the director and H.H. sipping whiskey and talking about good old Mourad, caught red-handed stealing office equipment. I see them loosening their ties, kicking back and calling in two girls to watch a porno film together. They hold their little orgies in H.H.'s bachelor flat, which is equipped with every comfort. One day he took me there to give me an idea of what I was missing, of what I could have if I were more flexible, more conciliatory. Two or three porno magazines were on the floor and a stack of hundred-dirham bills on the night table. I imagine them fornicating without a care in this apartment, its walls lined with cork so as not to disturb the neighbors.

They've cut some deals and gotten rich, but they could have gotten richer if I hadn't been in their way. They had simply brushed aside this grain of sand. But what they wanted was to brush him aside definitively. Hence this typewriter business. I could tell the judge everything. But I have no proof, and they would sue me for libel. What do I have to lose? A few months' suspended prison sentence? A reprimand from the administration? A dismissal, a pink slip, banishment, the loss of my civic rights, which means I would be barred from running for office and from voting? The entire apparatus could join forces against me at any time, the moment to be chosen by the justice system and the men who pull the strings. I imagine the machine going into motion and advancing in my direction to crush me. I imagine all this and more if I remain seated here, doing nothing, waiting for the trap to close around me.

That evening, I tell Najia everything. Afterward, she sighs and tells me:

"Being innocent isn't enough. Nor is being in the right. The law is never applied in full strength. Your story is of no interest unless it serves to implicate the corruptors and the corrupt. You played a role in this affair. You could give back the money and put corruption in this country on trial. But for that you need broad, solid shoulders, you need to be more than one person, you need... you need... But our voice isn't heard, it doesn't carry very far. We're not big enough to fight these cold, cynical monsters who are capable of rolling over us in their fits of laughter."

Then I tell her about the love story between Olivetti and Larousse. She laughs. She considers them an interracial couple capable of making great magic. She suggests I share my misadventures with the typewriter and is certain it will turn out a tale of the miseries and injustice of our times. When I think about it, I believe it. After all, being under the weight of the bed and the dictionary, under the immense weight of the French language especially, this typewriter is capable of providing the key to escaping this impasse. I have to try, to see what it has spit out since yesterday. Maybe it's doing Wassit's homework.

The love story between Olivetti and Larousse is my secret garden, my pleasure, my fantasy, my distraction. Since I discovered this relationship, I go into Wassit's room every day, lock the door, sit on the floor, and wait to read what the two of them have been writing at night. In the beginning, the sentences were confused. Words combined to form often incomprehensible expressions. From time to time, the title of a book emerged from the bowels of the typewriter. I gather these words and glue them together to form a little poem:

*Laughter is cruel*
*When the soul is suffering*
*When desire is impatient*
*And the sky mocking. . .*

Before leaving the room, I slip my white sheet of paper into the machine to make sure it is functioning. No one knows about this secret. I often tell myself that when strange things happen, you have to accept them as they are, without trying to explain everything. I know that intelligence is in comprehension of the world, it is the ability to surprise ourselves and realize that complexity doesn't explain obscurity. Those who demand absolute clarity are wrong or deluding themselves.

For now, I am at the point of dreaming the world, for want of transforming it. To dream is to assemble incongruous creatures and things and, based on them, to weave an ordinary or extraordinary story. I am only repeating Schopenhauer's idea, for whom "life and dreams are the pages of the same book; to read these pages in order is to live; to read them out of order is to dream."

For a long time I wanted to follow things in order. Now, and thanks to the Olivetti-Larousse affair, I am more trusting of dreams and disorder.

I SUDDENLY FEEL NOSTALGIC FOR THE QUIET BOREDOM OF those holidays when I was the only one who didn't find amusing the killing of a sheep in memory of Abraham's readiness to sacrifice his son. In my parents' house was a folkish drawing of an angel descending from the sky, a lamb in his hands, heading toward Abraham, an old bearded man, his knife poised at the throat of the poor adolescent... There was nothing amusing in this scene except perhaps for the angel, neither man nor woman, who flew in the sky, a little like Superman, whom we would later see at the movies flying to avenge the widow and the orphan. This quiet boredom is a state of mind and body that resembles a kind of calm, when there is nothing to do or prove. Everything moves in slow motion as others run about, laugh, shout instead of talking, eat too much and too fast, feel happy to be together, congratulate one another, love one another, detest one another, and pretend to be contributing to the collective happiness by their mere presence.

As a child, I would retreat to the terrace and tend to the silkworms I was raising in a shoebox. From the courtyards and patios rose the sounds and clamor of the celebration, lightened and somehow transformed. Meanwhile I felt quietly bored and let myself drift into insignificant daydreams.

Why do I feel this nostalgia today? I would like to become that child on the terrace again, withdrawing into his universe where no one is chasing him. We all need a little place on the terrace of childhood, where we are out of reach, almost as if we were dead.

NAJIA ADVISES ME TO GO HOME AND TALK TO MY WIFE. I know she's right. I also know it's pointless. Words have long ceased to connect Hlima and me. A mini-war has taken hold, undermining our interactions. I have wanted to strangle her so many times; each time I held myself back. Anyway, domestic violence is often committed by the weak. I know I'm a bit weak but I resist. When she talks, she screams. When she defends herself, it's in bad faith; she lies and curses. All this comes from a lack of education. Her mother raised her with only one goal in mind: to satisfy her selfishness and crush the weak. I don't feel like talking to her; indifference is my only defense. I'll take advantage of her absence to read and decipher the typewriter's messages. That will be my distraction and my secret. I still have a few days before the judicial machine starts up. First the disciplinary committee has to meet, and then refer the matter to the law courts. For the moment, I've only received a warning.

OLIVETTI AND LAROUSSE MUST HAVE HAD A FIGHT LAST night. The words are illegible and the paper is crumpled. I bend over to see if a mattress spring isn't sticking out and discover a nest of mice hidden in the corner. The mice eat paper. The dictionary, in fact, is full of holes; the typewriter is no longer the only one making beautiful sentences with it. I try arranging a few slips of paper end to end and, lo and behold, the magic couple makes poetry.

"Seasons betrayed, a time of lassitude on the back of thoughts... Dreams written by the lost sleep of a man stalked by the encroaching walls..."

Erased words, a collection of numbers and periods. I cover the typewriter with an old Chinese cloth and watch television, waiting for Hlima and the children to return. Images follow one after the next and nothing sticks in my mind. It's like an absurdist film in which the reels have been reversed. I think of the millions of Moroccans who, like me, are sitting across from their televisions, absorbing images without asking themselves any questions. Perhaps that's what our television is designed for. Actually, I watch and see nothing. Mud. Haze. Overlapping, infinitely multiplying images. Then I drift into my favorite exercise: imagining. I imagine myself. Alone. With neither wife nor children. Without Hlima, I feel happy and free. Without Karima and Wassit, I feel sad. But are they happy? The boy doesn't talk much. He's preparing for his exams under the lampposts on the avenue: that's all I know about his life. He works hard and makes himself scarce.

Karima understands everything and is more vulnerable. It's mostly for her that I came back home.

Self-imposed solitude is an acute form of selfishness, a refuge for those who feel unconcerned by the bustle we sometimes confuse with life. Deliberate solitude is a retreat to spare oneself a hard fall and even harder suffering. But isn't it contradictory to want to live without suffering? At the beginning of our marriage, I shared my thoughts with Hlima on life, death, and happiness. For her it was all some kind of madness. Everything is simple. Why work so hard at life? Soon she ceased to be a friend, a confidante, a partner. At the office I was just as alone. Who could I talk to? With whom could I share my disillusionment? I remember one evening I read her this thought of Schopenhauer's: ". . . pleasure is a thin film on a deep deposit of bitter sediment: joy is imprisoned, the finest sentiments conceal a hideous worm, mediocrity is a cruel Lent, glory martyrdom, obscurity a scourge, habit an inevitable plague that dulls all sensuality, but which sharpens and aggravates the edges of pain." I can still hear her deep chuckle, quoting in her own defense her mother's highly realistic philosophy: "There's no room in life for the weak, no mercy for the poor whose poverty is their own fault. You have to know how to fight. There's no pity for those who hesitate, no time to waste with those who philosophize or write poetry. Life is hard and you have to be hard. Unfortunately, I'm not hard enough. I used to pity you, you seemed so lost. I was wrong to have pity. Men like you would do better to remain alone. They would disappear and no one would even notice. Besides, what difference does it make whether you exist or not? You went to school, you have degrees, you have a library that you care for better than you do your children, and you work in an office where your assistant is the one who reaps all the benefits. You sign, and he pockets the commissions, builds a nice house, takes his wife and children on vacation..."

I don't like her voice. I don't know how to describe it. A harsh voice? No. Sometimes it's shrill, sometimes husky. It's strange, it's a voice that squeaks, scrapes, and hurts the ears. It also hurts my skin. The voice is affected by what it conveys, it's as unpleasant as the thoughts it speaks. It's unharmonious.

It's a voice that corresponds entirely to her temperament. But what is Hlima's temperament? For a long time I forbade myself from asking this question. What's the point of wondering about something you know in advance to be bad or harmful? It's no use pointing out to people their faults or their mistakes. Changing for them is the worst kind of torture, no one wants to change. I can't see Hlima waking up one day determined to change her behavior, not to mention her thoughts. Mediocrity is a cozy bed. It's easy to get used to it; you have pleasant dreams inside and you think you're better and stronger than other people. Hlima got the wrong man and she's mad. I also got the wrong wife, the wrong life. I've thought of suicide and have no excuse for not having done it. When I think of choosing death, my will to change my way of life asserts itself. I find the conditions under which I have been given to live deplorable, and when I think of destroying my body, it's not that I don't want to live, but that I don't want to live as Hlima does, following the examples of my assistant and my boss. But are they worth taking so seriously, is it worth dying because of the nauseating stench of their mediocrity? I know and like to repeat that "pleasure is a thin film on a deep deposit of bitter sediment." So why try to change others?

I think of Nadia, the girl with the glass eye. I think of that strange encounter, like a scene from a French film in black-and-white from the fifties. There is hidden distress in that woman's life.

I think of her as my female counterpart. Our wounds are different but our suffering traces the same path in our souls. When she makes love, she closes her eyes and gives herself slowly and sweetly. She loves to curl up against me and cry in silence. She'd rather be caressed than penetrated. "Caress me as long as you can," she tells me, "until your hands and skin get tired. Caress me slowly, I need it so much, you're like me, wounded, don't stop, give life to my skin, give air to my lungs. My body is yours, make it happy. Your hands are soft and firm. Leave your body on top of mine for a moment, rest. Leave your penis between my buttocks. Don't move. Let it warm up. Put your lips on the nape of my neck. I'm yours. Be gentle with my back. Don't think about your life. Do as I do, empty your mind of all the clutter. We're friends because we're alike and different. I was humiliated by men and refused all contact with them for a long time. I haven't made love in over a year. Luckily, you get used to it and you lose even the memory of pleasure. I'm talking to you just the way I talk to myself. At times I've caressed myself and felt pleasure mixed with shame. Caress me, give me pleasure and only pleasure. Then I'll get on top of you, you'll close your eyes and my mouth will travel all over your body. Afterward I'll harvest your semen and sleep beside you. You'll go away softly, without waking me, like a dream, night's gift to the day."

CORRUPTION HAS CHANGED MY LIFE COMPLETELY; IT caused me to meet Nadia, propelled me into the arms of my cousin and opened my eyes once and for all to Hlima and her entourage. Why should I complain? I'm not even suspected of having taken dirty money. They're only talking about an old typewriter. Perhaps it's more serious to steal—in my case, to borrow—office property than it is to take an undisclosed commission for signing a document. So I discovered that for years H.H. was selling my signature. He was negotiating with contractors, while I was signing with my heart and soul in good conscience. I can understand that he wants to do away with this intermediary. He took his perversion to the limit: he succeeded in making me cave in. Of course, Hlima and her mother supplied a lot of the pressure. I took some money. Twice I tasted forbidden fruit. I found a small degree of pleasure in it, then I was stricken with remorse. I tried to turn around, and that's when the trap snapped shut. This business about the typewriter is irrelevant. It's a pretext, a symbol, a signal. I can't even give it back. If I tell them what's going on between the typewriter and Larousse, they'll think I'm crazy. I'm keeping it to myself, for my moments of fantasy. What will they do to me? If I had taken big commissions I would have become a respectable man. But despite my corruption, I've remained small. And the small are crushed.

If I go to prison, I'll take Olivetti and Larousse with me. I'll tell them my story and they'll write it out. I'm sure they'll turn it into an unusual novel. The main thing is that my situation be clear.

$\mathcal{M}$Y STORY IS NOT OVER. I DON'T REALLY KNOW THE ending. I am writing it as things happen, which is why it's in the present. Maybe by writing it down the facts will take an unforeseen turn, maybe the words themselves will act on its evolution. If at the end of this story I am free, it will be thanks to the support of words. For the moment, I'm waiting. I don't have the right to return to the office, or to cross the border. I need my director's authorization to leave the country. They're scaring me, testing me. All this was put together by H.H. I'm so naïve. Now I understand why the bank tellers intimidated and blackmailed me. They're his friends, his accomplices. I understand the typewriter business. I should never have borrowed this old thing, which was serving no purpose. This is H.H.'s way of sending me signals: get in line, stop being a nuisance, get rich and let him do the same, and more; but if I insist on remaining honest, he'll make me pay. He has his ways.

I'm not moving. I'm sitting in an armchair whose springs are piercing my back and buttocks and I can't seem to get up. It's the effect of the television images; I'm going to wait until the end of the program and maybe then I'll be freed. It's hard to raise my arm; it falls back down like a heavy object, and I have just as much trouble moving my legs. I'm immobilized. I call Hlima, Karima, Wassit. My voice remains a prisoner at the bottom of my throat. It's like in a nightmare, when you scream and no one hears you because nothing comes out. I am trying to lift a cigarette butt to my mouth. Impossible. On television it is time for the reading of the Koran. I watch the verses parading across the screen. It's the sura on Cheating: "It was He that created you: yet some of you are unbelievers while others have faith. God is cognizant of all your actions… Those who disbelieve and deny Our revelations shall be inmates of the Fire, and shall abide therein forever: an evil fate."

Why doesn't Najia come save me? Why doesn't Nadia hear my cries for help? Am I already "an inmate of the Fire"? Only the flames are missing. The program is over. I hear the national anthem. I try to lift my arm to salute. Impossible. It must be the revenge of my shaky patriotism. I'm nailed down. The images are gone, only lines forming blurry images appear. I open my eyes wide. I think I see H.H. in his gray suit. I think I recognize my boss, also in a gray suit. It looks as if they're in a courtroom, but it's only a hallucination. I am definitely at home sitting in front of a television that I can't turn off. I am waiting for my wife and children. I am waiting for Najia or Nadia. I am waiting for anyone, even the police, so long as they get me out of this chair. I feel a spring slide between two ribs on my left. I'm in pain. Another spring slips between two ribs on my right. I'm stuck. Blood flows slowly down my stomach and legs and falls in droplets on the floor. I press the arms of the chair with all my might and try to tear myself from the springs. I almost make it, but I fall back, my face covered in sweat, exhausted. Where is this force coming from that's holding me down? It's fear, cowardice, poverty. All my life I've kept to the side, sought the happy medium, the thing that pleases everyone, the lukewarm option that doesn't hurt anyone, the consensus with no violence, no brutality, no passion. I have always had a hard time making decisions, settling matters. I like life or others to decide for me. I resisted corruption as much as I could, until the day I gave in to the pressure. That's why I'm in this situation today. I don't like conflicts or fights.

I am stupidly pacifist. I recognize that now. Is this the moment to be self-critical? I am alone, abandoned, isolated. Perhaps Hlima is behind the television screen, watching my suffering. But where are my children? Wassit must be under the street-lamp. Karima must be sleeping at her grandmother's. I am conjecturing all this to give myself a little hope. I am dreaming. But how can it be that I am dreaming in the dream, that I am watching myself dreaming and suffering, placed in this armchair by cruel hands, held here by an invisible force until the arrival of the flames?

I mentioned earlier the possibility of suicide. Fortunately, I didn't act on it. A person who commits suicide is cursed. His punishment is not only hell but his suicide repeated indefinitely. That's what religion says. I imagine myself as a resuscitated hanged man, performing the same gestures over and over again, looking for a solid rope, a stool, a hook somewhere. A hand, each time a different one, would pass me the rope. Sometimes it would be Hlima's hand, sometimes her mother's. H.H. would bring me the stool, assuring me it was sturdy. The boss would tell me where the hook was. All these hands would help me climb up on the stool, place the rope around my neck, and attach it to the nail. Hlima would be the one to kick the stool. She'd do it violently with all her strength. The rope would squeeze my neck and Hlima would come to make sure I was dead. First, she'd open my fly and slip her hand inside my pants to check if I had an erection; apparently hanged men get hard-ons at the moment of death.

The next day, I would go through the same ordeal with the same actors, except that the final blow would be struck by H.H., who, just prior to the hanging, would have sex with Hlima while the director filmed the scene.

No, hell must be far worse. As for suicide, I won't give my wife or my enemies such a gift.

In the situation I'm in, everything scares me, especially the threats of religion. I'm not seeing things clearly. It is neither the moment to doubt nor to revolt.

All this because I'm tired, terribly weary. I close my eyes and fall into a deep sleep. I am naked under a magic moon, walking on a white earth, followed by my shadow, which, from time to time, gets ahead of me and talks. I don't understand everything it tells me, but according to its gestures I know it wants to put me on guard against someone or something. I see a spider descending from the moon, but I'm not afraid. I continue forward until my shadow steps in front of me and prevents me from going any farther. I have an inkling it's the spider that feeds off the world; it descends once a year, on a full moon, grabs up a few desperate souls, then vanishes at the first rays of daylight. I ask myself: Are you ready? And my shadow answers for me, shouting a "No" that wakes me up.

*T*TOLD YOU THAT HLIMA'S VOICE WAS UNPLEASANT. I forgot to specify that it's loud. She is capable of waking the dead. From the depths of my strange sleep, I hear her. Hlima doesn't talk, she roars. It's her nature, her way of being in the world. The power of her voice gets the better of her and sometimes gives her away. She's the one who tears me from the armchair. She lifts me up and flings me against the mirror. I'm groggy. The shock is terrible. I lift my hand to my head and feel a lump. It's even bleeding a little, but I have no time to wipe it off. A thundering "Out!," repeated louder and louder, emerges from her furious mouth. Whatever else she says is nearly incomprehensible, but I realize it's the same old story, words like "incompetent, miserable, pathetic, bane of my existence, ball and chain, big nobody, weakling, penniless cheapskate, laughingstock..." During the avalanche of insults, despite the pain in my head and the numbness in my limbs, I am reminded of Murnau's film *The Last Laugh*, which stars that impressive actor Emil Jannings, who was the professor in *The Blue Angel*. A man is a porter in a luxury hotel. One day, he is fired for no known reason. Unable to admit to his wife and children that he has lost his job, he continues wearing his uniform and going off every morning as before. He stands near the hotel and watches his replacement at work. I don't remember the film at all, but the image of this man running after his dignity is fixed in my mind. Maybe I too will pretend to go to the office. I hope I don't sink so low. I won't let them have the last laugh; I won't prove my wife right, or make Karima cry.

I prefer to be on the street than to have to answer her questions. It's nice out. I head toward the boulevard. Maybe I'll meet Wassit under a streetlamp; it's not so late. I feel like walking, like being alone and not talking. I could also get a simple room in a simple hotel, a clean hotel with no stars, a hotel called "Terminus," the kind you find in every city that has a train station. But I don't want to hear the sounds of the cars changing tracks. I don't want to hear the wheels squeaking, metal rubbing against metal. That would disturb me and remind me of the voice of my wife, who is no longer my wife in reality but who is still present because I am weak and haven't managed to break all ties with her. I am afraid that the humiliation will be even greater, more flagrant. My fears are not at all logical. They're just there, hanging around me, grabbing my neck and strangling me until I lose my voice and my breath. Fear is an illness, passed on from father to son. It has been pursuing me since elementary school. I'd be furious if I happened to bequeath it to my son. For the time being, I don't think he's fearful, but rather courageous and clever. He's a son I barely saw grow up. He's always been independent. I'm not worried about him. Like me, he harbors a healthy anger. He can't accept injustice and rebels against humiliation. He tells me he'll fight for a better world. He wants to break out; he has a thirst for learning and a passion for freedom. I don't know what he'll do later on. He's talking about going into international relief work to help abused children. He says he'll start his activities in our neighborhood. He's right. People have too many children in this country, then take little and poor care of them.

I'm going to walk a little more. As they do every night, the cats are fighting over the garbage that litters the street corners. It stinks. A man is urinating against a wall. He's not a bum. He zips his fly, gets on his bicycle, and disappears into the night; this man's mission must be to water the neighborhood's building stones, and he's hitting every street. That's the way the city is, dirty and neglected where the poor live, clean and groomed in the better residential neighborhoods. A mini-taxi slows down next to me. The driver leans out and offers me a hotel room and a girl. He takes me for a tourist. I say no. He insists and tells me her name is Scheherazade and that she's right out of *The Arabian Nights*. I smile. He describes her: eyes big as the sea, breasts heavy as the sky, long, long hair... Then he gets discouraged and goes away. I think about this woman. What is she really like? Overweight, or just ordinary?

It dawns on me that there are very few public gardens in this city. The trees have been cut down to make room for buildings. Only the houses of real estate speculators are surrounded by trees and flowers. I would like to sit on a bench and stop thinking about all this. But there is no bench, so I keep walking. I'm already at the shore. The wind is cool. The sound of the sea does me good. I feel like smoking a cigarette opposite the white ocean waves. There's a bench, but I'm cold. The cigarette burns quickly. A boat passes in the distance. I resume my stroll. I'm happy to be alone. Suddenly I have a brief but intense sensation of being a happy man. The sensation is fleeting. I am escaping reality. I bid farewell to everything that holds me back; I even forget my children's faces. I am far away. I have become a stranger. It's terrible and wonderful. I don't care what happens anymore. Like the Sufi mystics, I am "renouncing." I am flying. I disappear. I am no longer a part of this harsh and mediocre world. I am above it. My feet no longer touch the ground and my head is already in the clouds. My body is carried by the wind, surrounded by words and syllables. I feel safe and have no need to return to earth.

This town is full of echoes. Some are always present, in the air, carried by the airwaves. I pass through them and hear their whistling. I bump into a wall of echoes, an old wall holding captive the sounds of another era.

In the shantytowns of the big city, women pray before curved mirrors. Their prayers hit the glass and turn to ashes, raining on their knees. They perceive life in a dazed stupor, their beliefs based on the smoke of incense. From high above where I am flying I hear them and laugh. The sky gives nothing, not even rain; it's stingy and indifferent to the faces turned toward it. What punishment to be so lucid as to find unexpected justifications for society's ugliness. The ugliness of the century, the ugliness of men, the ugliness of death.

Is night delivering me from the greatest anxiety, or is death relieving me of a heavy load?

I sense that I will have to touch down on solid ground. It's dawn. The light is soft. It's a bit cold. I'll go wash up at Najia's. She's still sleeping. I enter through the half-open window without waking anyone. I take a burning-hot shower, then a cold one. I feel different, like a brand-new man. I look in the mirror and barely recognize myself. The white spots have disappeared from my face; only a few remain under my arms. They were a warning after a shock. Now I've broken the force of the shock and the test. I rummage though Najia's closet where she keeps her husband's clothes. I borrow a beautiful suit, a white shirt, and a stunning tie. I make myself into a new man. I polish my shoes, open *Being and Nothingness* and take the remaining banknotes. I make some coffee and bring it to Najia. She's surprised to see me in her husband's clothes; she's afraid but then she smiles. I tell her I've decided to go back to the office. I've done nothing wrong. She doesn't quite believe me. She tells me she's not my mother. I kiss her and hold her in my arms. Her body is warm. She stands on the bed. I put my head on her stomach and her hands reach around me. She leans toward me and I notice a tear on her cheek. I tell myself I shouldn't have worn her husband's suit. But no, I have no regrets. He died a long time ago. A new life is beginning, without scruples or remorse. At that very instant I think of my death. It will be ordinary. I think of the insects that will eat my liver, my lungs, my heart. I think of my father, now only bones in the grave. All these images parade by in a few seconds. When I kiss Najia's moist lips, I feel a terrible desire to live.

I go outside, take a taxi to the office, and leave the driver a good tip. When the *chaouch* sees me, he stands at attention and salutes as if I were a superior officer. A secretary smiles at me and says:

"You smell good, Mr. Mourad!"

A colleague stops and shakes my hand.

Upon entering the office, I notice an old typewriter sitting on the floor.

"Why did you bring back this useless old thing?" the new secretary asks me. "It wasn't worth the trouble."

I'm surprised. I didn't bring anything back. I smile and say nothing. I bend over to see what it looks like up close. It's not an Olivetti, but a Remington. The whole thing was only a plot. I feel relieved. On my desk, the files have been laid out in order. The secretary remarks that in my absence the requests for construction permits have been flooding in.

H.H. arrives, smiling and warm. He kisses me as men do in Morocco. He smells good, too.

"So, are you feeling better? How was your little week of rest? You needed it. The boss and I were saying, 'He has to stop, he works too much, he's going to overdo it and we won't have the benefit of his services anymore!'"

I thank him. He comments that the typewriter on the floor is in the way and asks the secretary to put it in the back closet. When we're alone, H.H. looks at me, smiles, and says: "Welcome to the tribe!"

PARIS / BUBIÓN
FEBRUARY-OCTOBER 1993